The Disappearing Desert Kittens

The Disappearing Desert Kittens

by Ben M. Baglio

Cover art by Andrew Beckett
Interior art by Meg Aubrey

CANCEL

SCHOLASTIC INC.

New York   Toronto   London   Auckland   Sydney
Mexico City   New Delhi   Hong Kong   Buenos Aires

ISBN 0-439-79252-5

Text copyright © 2005 by Working Partners Limited.
Illustrations copyright © 2005 by Scholastic Inc.

All rights reserved. Published by Scholastic Inc.

SCHOLASTIC and associated logos are trademarks and/or
registered trademarks of Scholastic Inc.

12 11 10 9 8 7 6 5 4 3 2 1   5 6 7 8 9 10/0

Printed in the U.S.A.
First Scholastic printing, November 2005

To the real Jim and Jane Tatford, with love

Special thanks to Lucy Courtenay

Chapter One

Andi Talbot took the small, square present from under the twinkling Christmas tree and placed it in her mother's hands. "I was saving this until last, Mom," she said. "It's from me and Buddy. Merry Christmas!"

The little tan-and-white terrier sitting at Andi's feet barked when he heard his name. Judy Talbot carefully unwrapped the gift. "Oh, Andi!" she exclaimed, staring at the plum-colored velvet notebook. "I need a new diary for the new year, and this will be perfect. And it's my favorite color!" She reached over and hugged Andi tightly. "I can't believe you're going away for a week tomorrow," she said. "I know you'll have a wonderful time with your dad in Arizona, but Buddy and I are really going to miss you."

Andi swallowed a lump in her throat. "It's only a week, Mom," she said. "I'll be back before you know it."

She hadn't seen her dad since the fall and couldn't wait to spend some time with him — but it was so difficult to leave her mom and Buddy and her friends Tristan and Natalie behind.

"Don't worry about us," Mrs. Talbot said, reading the expression on Andi's face. "You just enjoy every second with your dad. I can't wait to hear all about Tucson when you get back."

"I'll send e-mails," Andi promised. "And you can use your new diary to write down everything while I'm away. I want to know what Buddy is up to, and whether you see Natalie and Tristan, and what the weather's like. So when I come home, it'll be like I haven't missed anything at all!"

The doorbell rang, making Buddy jump up and start barking. Andi shushed him and ran to open the door. Natalie Lewis was standing on the porch, wearing a stylish trilby hat in red leopard-print fur and a pink suede jacket.

"Merry Christmas!" she grinned, twirling to show off her new clothes. "Neat outfit, don't you think? I know the hat doesn't really match the jacket, but I couldn't decide which one I wanted to wear first. They'll both look so great with my chaps the next time we go riding!"

Andi's dad had recently given her some riding lessons

at the Hollow Creek Riding Center just outside Orchard Park. Natalie had joined in after getting to know Neil O'Connor, whose mom ran the center.

"You'll definitely be bright enough to spot in the forest," Andi teased. "Come in. I want to show you my new sneakers and this awesome bag Mom bought me for my trip."

"Did you pack already?" Natalie asked, sinking into the Talbots' couch. "I'm so jealous. You're going to get a great tan." She bent down and examined the pale skin on her legs. "I look like I've been under a rock."

The doorbell rang again. "Tristan's here!" Andi's mom called.

Tristan Saunders pulled off his green striped hat and ran a hand through his bright red hair as he came into the living room. "Merry Christmas, guys! I would have been here sooner, but it took us forever to finish dinner. Dean's pecan pie needed so much chewing, my jaws are tired!" He slumped dramatically onto the sofa next to Natalie. "Okay, I want to hear everything about this trip — especially the part about the snakes you're gonna see."

"It's winter in Arizona, too, you know," Andi pointed out. "The snakes will be asleep."

"Well, I hope you wake up a few," Tristan said. "You can't go all the way to Arizona and not see a rattlesnake."

Natalie rolled her eyes at Andi. Tristan had developed a passion for reptiles after helping out at the Orchard Park pet store, Paws for Thought. Sometimes it felt like he'd rather have scales than skin.

"Imagine," Tristan went on wistfully, "real live rattlers all around you. You'll practically be able to pick them up, there'll be so many."

"Thanks for that information, Tris," Andi said dryly. "I'll mail you one instead of a postcard. Or how about I bring home a boxful for your New Year's Eve party?"

Natalie threw a rubber bone for Buddy, and he brought it right back to Andi, as if he somehow knew it would be a while before he played with her again. She reached down and scratched his soft brown ears. *I'll miss Nat and Tristan, but I'll miss you most of all, Bud*, she thought.

"You'll walk Buddy every day, won't you?" she anxiously asked her mom. "He'll get fat with all the leftover turkey."

Judy Talbot smiled. "Of course."

Tristan picked up some photos that were lying on the coffee table. "Is this your dad's condo?" he asked, admiring the bright and sunny interior. "It looks awesome. I can't believe he found a place so quickly."

"Dad can't believe it, either," Andi admitted. "One

minute he was on an oil rig in the South China Sea, and the next he was told he had to be in Tucson in two weeks. He said that without the Internet to keep him in touch with his real estate agent, he'd be living in a tent right now!"

"Hey, you could have ended up camping," her mom joked, scooping up the torn wrapping paper and heading for the kitchen. "People pay good money for vacations like that."

Andi's parents were divorced, and her dad spent most of his time traveling around the world for his job. He and Andi's mom were still friends, and he sent them postcards of all the places he visited. He hadn't worked back in the States for as long as Andi could remember, but he'd come home to advise an Arizona-based firm on importing and storing fuel. Tucson wasn't exactly around the corner from Orchard Park, the suburb of Seattle where Andi and her mom lived, but it was a whole lot closer than the South China Sea!

Natalie and Tristan went home only after Andi had promised to e-mail every day she was gone. She went to help her mom unload the dishwasher, and as she stacked the dishes in the cupboard, she stared out of the window at the backyard. Everything here was so white and crisp and cold — the way the storybooks always said Christmas should be. Andi had loved every minute of it: the snowy mountains, singing carols while wrapped up in her mom's cozy red scarf, hot apple cider warming her cold fingers, the smell of pine needles, and crackling logs in the fireplace. The holidays here had been very different from holidays back in Florida, where they used to sit on the sun deck eating cold turkey sandwiches and watching the sun set over the sea. She wondered what Christmas in Arizona would be like. Hotter than Florida, probably. Suddenly she felt a rush of excitement and almost dropped the dish she was holding. In less than twenty-four hours, she'd be on her way to Arizona to see her dad!

"Ladies and gentlemen, this is your captain letting you know we'll be landing in ten minutes." Andi pulled off her headphones and listened as the voice crackled through the cabin. "Please fasten your seatbelts, and flight attendants, prepare for landing."

She peered out of the plane window as they started to descend. The landscape had changed dramatically since they'd left Washington State. The strong desert colors almost hurt Andi's eyes — reds and oranges and yellows set against a deep blue sky.

The plane landed with a tiny bump and taxied to a

halt. Shouldering her bag, Andi followed Marie, the flight attendant who had been assigned to take care of her, out to the waiting bus and then across the warm tarmac to the terminal. After Andi had passed through security and collected her luggage, Marie said good-bye with a smile. Andi checked her watch, then looked around for her dad.

"Chauffeur service for Andi Talbot," said a deep voice behind her.

"Dad!" Andi squealed.

"I can't believe you got so big!" David Talbot said, giving her a warm hug. "I swear you've grown since the fall. What's your mom feeding you?"

"Plant food," Andi joked.

"Let me get a good look at you." Her dad put his hands on her shoulders and stared at her. "You look pale," he said finally. "The Arizona sun will fix that!"

Andi looked up at him. "And you're so tan!" she said. "I thought your job kept you too busy for sunbathing?"

"Let's just say I make the most of my downtime," her dad replied with a grin. He took Andi's hand and they headed out of the air-conditioned airport into the late afternoon light. It was sunny and warm, and not too hot — Andi's idea of a perfect day.

Her dad lived on the edge of town, about twenty minutes from the airport. Andi recognized the neat white condo from the photos right away. Hibiscus flowers drooped around the doorway and filled the air with fragrance. Palm trees shaded the gardens and there was an inviting blue pool sparkling in the backyard.

Andi stood on the condo's doorstep and breathed in the warm, scented air. The sky was wide and clear, and dusty orange mountains stood far off in the distance, their shadows stretching across the desert as the sun sank lower in the sky.

"Do you like it?" Her dad was watching her.

"I'll get used to it, I suppose," Andi sighed.

Laughing, Mr. Talbot draped an arm around her shoulders and led her inside. The floor was covered with red terra-cotta tiles and brightly patterned rugs, and black-and-white landscape photographs hung on the pale walls. The living area was open, with large glass doors opening onto the back deck.

"What's my room like?" Andi asked.

"That's part of your Christmas present," said her dad. He opened a door at the end of the hallway to reveal a small white room with an arched window. Light from the setting sun streamed in and made patterns on the tiled floor. There was a bed and a chest of drawers, and a matching wooden desk in one corner with a computer sitting on it. The light was gorgeous, but the furniture was pretty bare. The room just didn't look cozy and lived-in like Andi's bedroom back home, where you could barely see the walls under all her animal posters.

"It's . . . er . . . great," Andi said.

"No, it's not," her dad countered, grinning. "It's a blank canvas. I wanted to wait until you got here and let *you* personalize it. I want you to feel like it's a real home away from home, and you're welcome here anytime. I'll take you shopping tomorrow. We can get rugs, pictures, lamps — anything you like."

Andi spun around and beamed up at him. "Anything? That's a *great* Christmas present! Thank you!"

"You bet," her dad said, dropping a kiss on her forehead. "We'll take a walk around town a little later, so you can get your bearings, and maybe we'll get some initial ideas for your room."

Automatically, Andi looked around for Buddy. If they were going out, he'd love to come, too. Then she remembered he was back in Orchard Park with her mom. Her excitement dimmed a little as she thought about Buddy and Tristan and Natalie back home. What if someone needed the Pet Finders while she was away? Andi had started the Pet Finders Club with Tristan and Natalie after Buddy got lost once. Thinking of her friends looking for missing pets without her suddenly made her feel strange.

"Are you okay?" asked her dad, looking concerned.

Andi forced herself to smile. "I'm fine. I was just thinking about the Pet Finders Club."

"I'm sure Orchard Park's missing guinea pigs can spare you for a week," her dad joked.

Andi frowned. "It's more than just guinea pigs, Dad," she said. "We've found reptiles and dogs, and a pedigree cat. We even found that pony that disappeared from the riding center, remember?"

"That's great, honey," Mr. Talbot said absently, heading into the kitchen. "Can I fix you a snack before we go out? You must be starving."

Andi was a little disappointed that her dad wasn't taking the Pet Finders seriously. *He doesn't mean to upset you*, she told herself. *He just doesn't understand how important it is*.

"Hey!" she exclaimed, distracted by the brightly decorated cactus standing in the corner of the room. She hadn't spotted it on the way in because it had been hidden behind the open door. "Is this your Christmas tree, Dad?"

Her dad passed her a sandwich across the breakfast

bar. "It's an Arizona tradition," he said. "We don't get fir trees around here, so we use what we have."

"Careful, you're already sounding like a local."

"I feel like one," her dad smiled. "I took this job because of the great vacations my family used to have in Arizona when I was a kid. It's always been a special place to me."

Nibbling on her sandwich, Andi examined the sparkling decorations hanging from the fat, prickly leaves of the cactus. There were stars, little colored lights, and a straw angel sitting on the top. It was cute and quirky, and Andi thought it was kind of cool.

Her dad jingled his car keys. "Ready? Let's go exploring!"

It was a short drive to the local shopping district. Andi's dad parked the car beneath a palm tree, and they walked down the street together, peering into the windows of the brightly colored stores: They were painted red, deep blue, and pink. Andi spotted rugs, jewelry, paper lanterns, and delicately woven baskets displayed in the windows. They passed food stores hung with strings of blazing red peppers, clothing boutiques with racks full of rainbow-knit clothes and soft scarves, furniture stores and astrology shops, book stores, and art galleries. Bright red buses rumbled past every few minutes, and the air was full of the smell of spice and dust and incense.

When they passed a pet store, Andi dragged her dad to a stop so she could get a good look. It reminded her of Paws for Thought. She took a deep breath of the familiar smell of sawdust and animal feed. Maybe she should go in tomorrow and introduce herself, just in case her pet-finding skills were needed while she was here!

"I'm going to get a newspaper," her dad told her, pointing to a store on the other side of the road. "I won't be long. Will you be okay waiting here?"

Andi nodded. "Sure."

Feeling as if she were missing an arm without Buddy, she looked around for people walking their dogs. The only animals she saw were a skinny sand-colored cat slinking down an alleyway and a gray dog walking slowly toward her. She reached out her hand and pet the dog on the head as he limped by arthritically.

"Hey there, old guy," she said, stroking the dog's raggedy ears. "You've found a nice place to retire, huh? Plenty of sunshine and plenty of people to talk to."

There was no sign of the dog's owner. Andi wondered if maybe he was lost or a stray. But the dog seemed perfectly content, as if he knew exactly where he was heading. He regarded Andi for a moment, then lowered his head and continued on his way. As Andi watched him go, she felt herself longing for Buddy. It looked like the people of Tucson weren't that crazy about pets. Maybe a place like this wouldn't need a Pet Finders Club at all!

Chapter Two

Dear Mom and Buddy,
I got here okay. The flight was cool, and Dad's house is great! He put a computer in my room so I can send you lots of e-mails (and get e-mails back, too, of course!). My room is plain white at the moment, but Dad says I can decorate it any way I want. We took a walk around town this evening, and you wouldn't believe how colorful everything is. I think I'm going to decorate my room in bright colors, like green and blue and yellow, to contrast with the red floor tiles. Dad's taking me shopping tomorrow.

Andi paused. She wanted a cactus in a deep blue pot so she could imagine being outside in the golden desert. She had seen some beautiful wall hangings and rugs in shades of reds and blues and yellows, and a stack of gorgeous green baskets that would look great on the shelves above the desk.

She turned back to the keyboard.

Does it feel strange at home without me? I hope Buddy's not missing me too much and is eating okay. Did you take him for a walk today? I only saw one dog in town tonight. I don't think people in Tucson have as many pets as we do in Orchard Park. In fact, there don't seem to be many animals at all! I haven't even seen a rabbit here for Buddy to chase. There are a few geckos, but I think they move too quickly for Bud.

A wave of homesickness hit Andi like a truck, and the computer screen went blurry. She wiped her eyes crossly. There was no way she wasn't having a great time. Her dad had taken her to a Mexican restaurant for supper. They'd listened to a mariachi band and browsed the little street stalls that had sprung up under the palm trees when the sun went down. There was so much to tell her mom, but all she could write was stuff about Buddy. What was wrong with her?

"You're just tired," she said out loud. It was true. She'd had a long day, and she'd been yawning ever since they left the restaurant. She turned back to the screen.

Time for bed. It's been a crazy day. Send me an e-mail as soon as you read this, so I get to read it first thing in the morning! I miss you and Bud tons.
Lots of love,
Andi xx

With a sigh, Andi sent the e-mail and logged off. Leaning on the windowsill, she stared out at the black desert. There was no moon tonight, and the air was sharp and cold. The lights of Tucson twinkled and glimmered, stretching away into the distance. Andi was struck again by how much bigger than Orchard Park it was. It felt kind of weird, being in a huge city out in the middle of nowhere! Yawning again, she got into her pajamas and padded to the bathroom to clean her teeth. After saying goodnight to her dad, she climbed underneath her quilt and lay on her back, gazing up at the ceiling and watching the shadow play of distant headlights dance across it until she fell asleep.

In the morning, it took Andi a few moments to figure out where she was. Outside the sky was blue and the air was already beginning to heat up. There was an appetizing smell wafting down the corridor from the kitchen.

"Breakfast in ten minutes!" her dad called. "Are you up yet?"

Andi jumped out of bed. "Do I have time to check my e-mail?" she asked, putting her head around her bedroom door.

"Sure," said her dad, expertly flipping a pancake. "Just remember that I might start eating yours."

There were two e-mails — one from her mom and one from Natalie. Curling her legs underneath her, Andi read the e-mail from her mom first.

You'll get this first thing in the morning, Andi — just like you asked! I'm okay and Buddy's doing fine. He ate a pair of your socks yesterday afternoon. I guess he missed the smell of your feet!

The rest of her mom's e-mail was full of stories about Buddy, and she'd signed off with five kisses at the bottom. Andi turned to the e-mail from Natalie. It was almost like having her right there in the room.

Yo, Andi!
Remember the set of obedience classes Mom gave Jet for

Christmas? We took Jet this afternoon. First, he wouldn't even go in the door. He just barked at all the other dogs trying to get to the class, like he was guarding the place or something. When he finally decided to go inside, he went straight up to Fisher. How cool is it that Fisher Pearce teaches Basic Obedience?! Jet really got into the lesson and even learned to sit on command!! I only had to lean on him a little to make him do it. He's so smart that he practiced all the way home, sitting down on the sidewalk and in the middle of the street even when I didn't ask him to!!!

Andi grinned. Feeling much more cheerful, she took a quick shower and pulled on a lightweight T-shirt and her favorite pair of cargo shorts. It seemed strange to put on summer clothes after all the warm layers she had to wear in Orchard Park this time of year.

"It sounds like this Fisher Pearce guy has his work cut out with Jet," Andi's dad observed when she told him about her e-mails. He put several pancakes on her plate, and they sat together in a sunny spot on the deck.

"If anyone can teach Jet, Fisher can," Andi told him, pouring a generous puddle of syrup on her pancakes. "He's the local ASPCA vet. We've gotten to know him pretty well through all our pet finding."

"You've gotten to know a lot of people through this pet finding stuff from the sound of it," her dad commented. "Didn't you meet Natalie that way?"

Andi nodded. "She's such a great friend. It's weird to think that I wouldn't have met her if our dogs hadn't been missing at the same time."

"Another missing-dog mystery, solved by Andi Talbot," her dad teased. "Orchard Park sounds like a pretty dangerous place for pets."

"Ha ha," Andi said, making a face at him. She was determined not to get upset by anything her dad said about the Pet Finders Club today.

"So, are you ready for our shopping spree?" Mr. Talbot asked her as they cleared the plates.

"You bet," Andi said, rinsing the frying pan and propping it beside the sink to dry. She scooped up her jacket and followed her dad to the door. "I saw some gorgeous stuff yesterday that I want to get a closer look at. I saw these beanbag chairs, and a horse poster, and a couple of rugs, and there was a great lamp in the window of one store — "

Mr. Talbot put up his hands. "I get the message," he said. "We'd better get started right away if we're going to buy the whole town!"

*   *   *

The shops were quieter than they'd been the night before, with only a handful of people browsing the stores. There was no sign of the mariachi band, and the restaurants had their shutters closed, although Andi thought she could still smell fajitas in the air. Stores had their doors wide open, with baskets and clothes displayed enticingly on the sidewalk. Andi ran her hand across a pile of rugs covered with intricate designs and admired a Navajo woman dressed traditionally in a velvet shirt, long skirt, and petticoats, with a colorful blanket around her shoulders like a poncho.

"Do you mind if we go in here?" Mr. Talbot pointed to a small art gallery hung with bright oil paintings.

Andi glanced in the window and suppressed a sigh. She wasn't quite as excited about art as her dad — she liked stuff that *did* something, like baskets to put things in, or rugs to keep your feet warm. She followed her dad into the gallery and waited while Mr. Talbot chatted with the owner. Andi wandered over to the wall opposite the door and stared at some red and black and green swirls that might have been running deer, or mountains at sunset, or maybe both.

"Sorry, Andi," her dad said, rescuing her after twenty minutes. "I got a little carried away talking to the owner. Don't you love this stuff?"

"It's interesting," Andi said, diplomatically.

"I used to love painting back in the day," her dad reminisced as they stepped back into the blazing sunshine. "I'm a little rusty now but maybe I could get some lessons. I love that abstract style."

Privately, Andi thought Buddy could have done better with his paws covered in paint. They walked along the sidewalk until they reached another gallery. This place had one enormous electric-blue painting hanging on the wall and nothing else.

At least Dad won't want to go in here, Andi thought. Across the street was the furniture store she'd seen the night before, with the colorful beanbag chairs stacked in the window. They were just the thing Andi wanted for her room.

"That's beautiful!" her dad exclaimed, staring at the giant rectangle of blue. "I've got to go in and ask about the artist."

"But Dad, you said we were shopping for me this morning!" Andi didn't want to sound selfish, but she couldn't face another twenty minutes of looking at pictures that didn't make a whole lot of sense to her.

"I won't be long Andi, I promise."

Andi stood in the doorway, half-wishing the blue painting would fall off the wall. After throwing several meaningful glances at her dad (who ignored them), she decided to stop wasting her morning.

"Is it okay if I go across the street to those stores, Dad?" she called.

"Hmm?" Mr. Talbot looked surprised, as if he'd forgotten she was there. "Sure, honey, go right ahead. I'll come find you."

With relief, Andi hurried out into the street. How could anyone talk for so long about something so . . . blue? Looking right, then left, she jogged across the street toward the store, which was painted a bright bubble gum pink.

Somewhere to her left, she heard a voice. "Sorry, fella, I didn't see you down there!"

Andi turned to see a man carefully stepping over a snoozing brown dog outside a canary-yellow store called Santa Rosa Crafts, several doors farther down the street. She realized the dog was the one she'd seen yesterday, ambling along in the evening sunshine. She decided to go over and say hello.

"Hi, boy!" Andi felt absurdly happy to see the dog again. He seemed to remember her, because he lifted his head in greeting as she came over to pet him. His coat was rough and flecked with grizzled white fur, and although Andi could feel his ribs as she petted him, he

wasn't overly thin. She gently ran her hand down his leg and picked up his paw to check underneath. His pads were tough, but not cracked like the pads of stray dogs who spent all their time on the street. It was clear he hadn't been living rough, which was a relief.

Straightening up, Andi looked through the store window and admired the rugs and wall hangings on display. Some beautiful baskets were stacked by the cash register, and there were several cabinets filled with carved wooden animals and glittering silver, amber, and turquoise jewelry. It looked like a great place to start hunting for accessories for her room.

A tiny high-pitched sound dragged Andi's attention away from decorating and made her glance around. It sounded like a kitten, but there wasn't any sign of cats in the street. Andi shook her head. Maybe she still had water in her ears from her shower.

"I can't help it," she told the old dog, giving him one last pat. "Even though I'm on vacation, I still think like a Pet Finder!"

The door to the craft store was open, and Andi stepped inside. Wind chimes tinkled softly somewhere over her head. The store stretched back quite a way, and she could see that there were more display cabinets and racks of brightly colored clothes at the back.

The air was filled with a spicy smell, and Andi spotted a coil of incense burning in a small earthenware pot beside the cash register. There was no sign of a salesperson.

A large rug lay spread out beside one of the cabinets. The woven colors seemed to glow like jewels, and Andi couldn't help noticing it was the perfect size for her new room. It had a pale, corn-colored background and a black border. In the middle there was some kind of plant — a cactus or an abstract tree — standing in a red pot. Yellow, gray, blue, and green birds flew around the branches in a whirl of activity. Andi crouched down and stroked the rug, feeling the warmth and texture of the wool. She glanced cautiously at the price tag and whistled between her teeth. It was way more than she could afford — at least three times her Christmas money. But there was something about the rug that made it hard for Andi to tear her eyes away.

The high-pitched yelping sound came again. Andi whirled around. This time she was sure she wasn't imagining things. The sound was much closer than it had been from outside. There were kittens in here! Her mind started racing. Were the kittens lost or trapped? Was their mother with them? She hadn't heard or seen any sign of an adult cat. Andi's pet-finding instincts kicked in. She started moving slowly around the store, peeking under tables and behind piles of cushions and rugs.

At last, she tracked the crying to a beautiful red-and-gold coiled basket sitting beside the cash register. Bending down, she carefully lifted the basket lid and peered inside.

"Oh, how cute!" There, curled in a heap of soft brown tabby fur, sat three tiny kittens.

Chapter Three

"I'm sorry, but the kittens aren't for sale."

Andi straightened up to see a girl standing beside the register. Her long black hair fell almost to her waist, and she was wearing a sea-green velvet tunic over a pair of slim-fitting pants. A chunky bracelet of silver and turquoise circled her wrist. She looked a couple of years older than Andi.

"Are they yours?" Andi asked.

"Not exactly. We're taking care of them for a while," the girl said. She came around to Andi's side of the counter and bent down to stroke the kittens' small, soft ears.

"I heard them meowing and thought maybe they were trapped or something." Andi suddenly felt silly. It was clear that the girl had known the kittens were in the basket all along.

The girl smiled, making her brown eyes look warm and friendly. "Don't worry about it," she said, scooping up one of the kittens. "It's nice you were concerned. I'm Nina Nelson, by the way. My grandfather owns this store. Are you visiting Tucson?"

"My dad lives here," Andi explained. "I just got here yesterday. My name's Andi. You have some great stuff," she added, looking wistfully at the jewel-colored rug. "Does your grandfather make the rugs?"

Nina shook her head. "Rug making is passed from mother to daughter in Navajo tradition," she said, tucking the pale tabby kitten under her chin, where it wriggled and purred impatiently until she distracted it with a strand of her hair. "My mom tried to teach me lots of times, but I was always better with animals than looms!"

"I'd be hopeless at weaving," Andi confessed. "I can't even braid hair. But I'm crazy about animals!"

The girls grinned at each other. There was something about the Navajo girl that immediately made Andi feel comfortable.

The kitten under Nina's chin yelped. "Hush, Dezba," Nina murmured, stroking one finger on the kitten's soft tabby head.

"That's an unusual name," Andi ventured. "Is it Navajo?"

Nina nodded, and gently replaced Dezba in the red-and-gold basket with her siblings. One of them reached out a paw and patted playfully at her tail. Without missing a beat, Dezba pounced on her assailant, who scrambled to the back of the basket.

"It means 'goes to war'," Nina said with a grin. "You can see she's pretty feisty!"

"What are the others called?" Andi reached into the basket and picked up a light brown kitten with huge yellow eyes. Very carefully, she cradled the tiny creature in her hands and held it up close to her face. The kitten shook its head and sneezed, then looked rather surprised.

"That one is Nascha," Nina explained. "You see how big her eyes are? Nascha means 'owl'."

Nascha closed her eyes and gave a tiny contented purr as Andi rubbed her ears.

"And the boy is Yas," Nina added, tickling the remaining kitten under his tabby chin. "He has splashes of white on his feet and his chest — see? Yas means 'snow'."

"I like that their names mean something," Andi said. "I have a dog called Buddy. I called him that because I knew right away he was going to be my best friend."

She was about to tell Nina all about Buddy and her

friends back home in Orchard Park when a sudden pounce from Dezba tipped the basket over. It tumbled onto its side and rolled over. Sensing freedom, the kittens squeaked and clambered over one another to reach the floor. Then, with their tails stuck straight out with excitement, they tumbled off in three entirely different directions.

"If we lose them in here, we might never find them!" Nina yelped, jumping to her feet. "Quick, Andi, help me catch them!"

Andi made a grab for Yas, but he dodged behind a pile of baskets. Dezba shot beneath one of the display cabinets, while Nascha darted for the door like a small brown arrow. Nina ran to the door and slammed it shut, forcing Nascha to skid to a halt and change direction.

Lying full-length on the ground, Andi peered underneath the cabinet where Dezba was hiding. She carefully reached a hand underneath and felt around for the kitten.

"Ouch!" Pulling back, she stared at the neat line of scratches on the back of her hand. A tabby paw shot out from under the cabinet and batted a small piece of fluff before disappearing again.

"That's nothing." Nina walked over with Nascha and

Yas in her arms and looked down at Andi's wounds. "It hurts much more when she bites your ankles. Once she's out, she's a real devil to catch. We could be here all day!"

"Hmm." Andi frowned. Dezba obviously had great hunting instincts. If she could find something to dangle for the kitten to catch, perhaps she could coax her out that way. Andi suddenly remembered the cords threaded through the hems of her cargo shorts. She tugged one out until it was long enough to reach the floor, and swung it lightly beside the cabinet. On cue, Dezba's paw flew after the cord, trying to snag it with her claws.

Andi moved the cord a little further away, and the paw stretched out after it. She shifted the cord a little more, and a pair of neat triangular ears appeared. . . .

Pawstep by pawstep, Andi lured the kitten out of her hiding place. When Dezba had almost completely emerged from beneath the cabinet, Andi let her sink her claws into the cord and scooped her up.

Nina whistled and looked impressed. "You must have had a lot of practice at this kind of thing!" she said.

Andi was about to explain about the Pet Finders Club when footsteps at the back of the store made them both look around. A tall man with long gray hair tied back

with a leather string was walking toward them. He was dressed in dark linen trousers and a collarless white shirt. A string of amber beads hung around his neck. Andi moved back to make room for him and bumped into the display cabinet, making the pieces of silver and turquoise jewelry shiver and tinkle.

"Please," the old man said in a low rumbling voice. "Don't look so worried. You are welcome in my store, as long as you don't break anything."

"She was rescuing Dezba, Grandfather," Nina explained.

Nina's grandfather frowned. "You and those cats!" he growled. "This is a store, not a zoo! Besides, where Dezba is concerned, it is usually the people who need rescuing, not the cat. So, who is your new friend, Nina?"

"Andi, this is my grandfather, Dakota Nelson," said Nina. "Grandfather, this is Andi."

"Andi," Dakota Nelson echoed, nodding. "And what is your family, Andi?"

"Do you mean my last name?" Andi asked, surprised. "It's Talbot."

"And your mother's name?" Dakota Nelson prompted.

"Uh, my mom's last name was O'Keefe before she married my dad," Andi said, not sure where the conversation was leading.

Dakota Nelson seemed satisfied. "Then you are born to the clan of O'Keefe," he said. "That is how the People would see you, anyway." He smiled at Andi.

"Navajos call themselves 'the People'," Nina explained. "I'm of the Bitter Water clan, but my grandfather is of the Deer Spring Clan. You always take the name of your mother's clan. When we meet others of the People, we always give our mother's and father's clan names. That way, everyone knows exactly who you are and where you come from."

"Wow," Andi said, impressed. "That must be pretty useful if you ever need to find someone." She thought of the times when she, Tristan, and Natalie had to hunt through phone books when they were Pet Finding. The Navajo way would be much easier!

"So, Andi of the clan of O'Keefe," Dakota Nelson said, folding his arms. "Do you see anything that you like in my store?"

"I love your beautiful bird rug," Andi confessed, helping Nina put the kittens back in their basket. "But to tell the truth, I like everything in here."

"That's good to hear," Dakota Nelson said. "Sadly, I don't think you are planning to buy everything, are you?"

Andi laughed. "I wish I could."

"Tell me if you want to see anything up close," said the old man, indicating the display cabinets.

"Oh, I don't want jewelry," Andi said. "I mean," she added hastily, "it's beautiful and everything, but I'm looking for things to decorate my new room."

A gasp from Nina made them look around. "Dezba's figured out how to climb out of the basket without knocking it over!" she told them, making a grab for the scruff of Dezba's neck.

"Take those cats out to the back and feed them, Nina," Dakota Nelson ordered. "I am tired of having them under my feet all the time. This is — "

" — a store, not a zoo. Yes, I know, Grandfather." Nina sighed as if she'd heard it a hundred times.

Andi helped carry the kittens to the back of the store. Nina pushed through a beaded curtain and Andi followed her into a warm, cluttered kitchen.

"Doesn't look like your grandfather likes animals very much," she remarked, as Nina opened the refrigerator and took out a bowl of kitten food.

"He worries about the customers thinking that his store is unprofessional," Nina said, setting the bowl on the floor. The kittens scurried over immediately. "But don't be fooled. I've seen him petting the kittens when he thought I wasn't looking."

Andi played with the tip of Dezba's tail as the bossy little kitten pushed her brother and sister away from the food. "What happened to their mother?" she asked.

"She's semi-feral," Nina explained, gently pushing Yas and Nascha up to the food bowl again. "She lives outdoors, and only shows up at the back gate for food sometimes. I couldn't believe it when I found her with a litter of kittens! It gets really cold at night, so I brought them inside. Mosi — that's what we call her, it means 'cat' in Navajo — stayed for a little while, but the desert called her back one day, and she disappeared."

"She abandoned her family just like that?" Andi was shocked and sad for the kittens.

"Wild cats make their own rules," Nina said. "It's hard to accept, but it's wrong to expect them to behave the same way as domestic cats. Mosi is clever. She knows that her kittens will be safer here than out in the desert while they're so young and vulnerable."

Andi hadn't thought of it like that.

"When they're older, they'll survive better in the wild because they'll be bigger and stronger," Nina continued. "It's an honor that Mosi thought we could raise her family for her, but it's hard work. She visits sometimes, but we never know when she's coming."

Andi heard her dad's voice in the store. She pushed back the beaded curtain and waved at him. "Hi Dad, I'm over here!" she said. "You'll never guess what I found!"

"Trust you to find animals on your first morning in Tucson," Mr. Talbot teased when she showed him the kittens. They were curled up in a tangled heap on one of the kitchen chairs, so close it was impossible to tell where one kitten ended and another began. "They're very cute, but they aren't exactly the kind of room accessories I had in mind."

"Don't worry, Dad, they're not for sale," Andi told him.

"Perhaps they should be," Dakota Nelson grumbled from the doorway.

"Don't be mad, Grandfather," said Nina, standing on tiptoe to kiss him on his weathered brown cheek. "Mosi will come for them one day soon, and then you won't need to worry about them any more."

"So, Andi, have you seen anything you like — apart from the kittens, I mean?" her dad asked.

Andi decided not to mention the bird rug. It was too expensive, and she didn't want to take advantage of her dad's generosity. "There are a couple of great baskets, and I love the incense burner by the register," she said.

"Let's get those then," Mr. Talbot said promptly.

Dakota Nelson rang up the purchases while Nina wrapped the incense burner in tissue paper. With her grandfather's permission, she added a free box of incense sticks — "to say thanks for catching Dezba," she explained.

"May I come back and see the kittens again?" Andi asked.

"Come any time," Nina said enthusiastically. "Hey, do you like riding?"

Andi beamed. "Horseback riding? I love it!"

"My mom runs a riding center just outside of town and takes people on trail rides through the desert," Nina explained. "Would you like to come with me this weekend?"

Andi's eyes widened. Trail riding in the desert sounded fantastic! "Can I, Dad?" she begged.

"Of course you can!" her dad smiled. "This is your vacation!" Andi beamed. "Hey, watch out!" Mr. Talbot warned as she narrowly missed knocking over a pile of baskets in her excitement. "You don't want to hurt yourself and not be able to ride — or decorate your room."

"What else are you doing to your room? Have you

thought about painting the furniture?" Nina asked, her eyes gleaming with interest.

"That's an idea." Andi said. "What color should I paint them?"

"You could try blue," Mr. Talbot suggested. "It's a popular color around here, and it would look terrific against the red floor and white walls. We can get some paint on the way home."

Andi glanced at the bird rug again. It would look amazing with the red tiles and the blue furniture.

Mr. Nelson saw where she was looking. "That is the tree of life," he said, leading Andi over to show her the details on the rug. "This is a cornstalk growing in a pot, with the birds of the air around it. There is a legend that says that the People were born from a cornstalk. And see this?" He pointed at a thin, pale line of wool leading to the edge of the rug's black border. "It is a spirit line. The weaver puts it in to lead her spirit back out of the rug and into the Universe. Without it, many weavers believe that their spirit will remain trapped in the rug forever."

Fascinated, Andi traced the spirit line with her finger. The rug was even more beautiful up close. She thought she recognized some of the birds — jays, cardinals, and woodpeckers. There were butterflies and flowers and vines woven around the base of the cornstalk, and the rug seemed to glow with life.

"I love it, but I don't think I can afford it," she said honestly.

Dakota Nelson smiled. "It is still a pleasure to tell you about the pattern," he said. "I will show you more another time."

Andi put her head through the curtain to say goodbye to the kittens and then headed outside with her dad, holding tightly to her paper bag. Nina and her grandfather followed them, talking about the window display. The ancient gray dog was still sitting outside the door. Instinctively, Andi glanced back at Mr. Nelson. He didn't seem to like having the kittens inside his store. What would he say about an old dog on his doorstep?

To her surprise, Nina's grandfather came out of the store and bent down to tickle underneath the dog's chin. He talked softly in a rhythmical language that Andi guessed was Navajo and ran his hands down either side of the dog's neck and his sides. The dog squirmed with pleasure and rolled onto his back, beating his long tail against the sidewalk.

"This is my dog, Tate," Mr. Nelson explained, standing up again. He had a gentle tone in his voice that Andi hadn't heard before. "He was a fine hunting dog in his day, but he's getting old now. These days he prefers sunbeams to rabbits and earns his keep by bringing customers into my store. Don't you, boy?"

Tate turned his head and gazed adoringly up at his master. Andi smiled to herself. It seemed that there was one rule for Mosi's kittens and an entirely different one for Tate!

Chapter Four

After going to a hardware store to buy a can of electric-blue paint and several brushes, Andi and her dad returned to the condo. Andi put her new baskets on the shelf above the computer and placed the incense burner on the windowsill. Then she and her dad carried her desk, chair, bedframe and bedside table out onto the deck. Andi put on an old shirt of her dad's, laid down a floor of old newspaper, and set to work, painting the bedframe first since it was the biggest. Soon her hands were blue with paint, from her fingertips to her wrists. The paint glowed in the bright desert light, and Andi felt a skip of excitement at the thought of the life her vivid furniture would soon bring to her little white room.

They had a snack while the first pieces were drying,

then set to work finishing the rest before the light faded from the sky.

"There!" Andi declared at last, leaning back to admire her handiwork. Her back ached and she was covered in blue paint, but it had been worth it. The furniture looked fantastic.

"You'll have to spend the night on your mattress on the floor," her dad advised, wiping his hands on a damp rag. "The paint needs to dry overnight."

"It'll feel like camping," Andi said, smiling as she remembered the conversation she'd had with her mom.

Then, as if she'd sensed Andi was thinking about her at that very moment, her mom called.

"Hey, Judy," Mr. Talbot said, cradling the phone under his chin. "Yes, we're doing great. Andi's right here, I'll hand you over."

"Are you okay, honey?" Judy Talbot sounded anxious on the other end of the phone. "You sounded homesick in your e-mail last night."

"Sorry about that, Mom," Andi apologized. "I was tired, and I really missed you and Buddy. But we had a great time today. I found some kittens. . . . "

"You're pet finding already?" her mom said, astonished.

Andi laughed. "Let me finish, Mom! The kittens

weren't lost. They belong to a really nice girl named Nina. Her grandfather owns this gorgeous Navajo store. I saw the old dog from yesterday again, because he belongs to Dakota — that's Nina's grandfather. And listen to this — I'm going riding in the desert on the weekend!"

"I thought you said Tucson didn't have any animals?" her mom exclaimed.

"Looks like I found them all in one day," Andi boasted. She told her mom all about her new baskets, the tree of life rug, and her furniture painting.

"Well, you sound like a different person today," her mom said when Andi stopped for a breath.

Andi moved the receiver to her other ear so she could wipe a blob of blue paint off her hand. "How's Buddy? Have you seen Natalie and Tristan?" she asked. "I've got so much to tell them."

"Buddy and I went for a long walk today," her mom said. "We met Natalie and Jet in the park. He kept sitting down in the middle of the grass and refusing to move. I think Natalie was getting frustrated."

"She's been taking him to obedience classes," Andi said. "I think Jet's taking the whole sitting thing a little too seriously. Hey, Mom, put Buddy on the phone, will you?"

She heard her mom calling Buddy and the distinctive scrabbling of the terrier's claws on the hall tiles. Suddenly she could hear Buddy's breathing loud and clear on the line. "Bud?" she said. "Hey, fella! Are you okay without me?"

Buddy started barking so loudly that Andi had to pull the phone away from her ear. "Shhh!" she protested from a safe distance. "Buddy, calm down!"

"He's going crazy," her mom warned, coming back on the line. "He can't figure out where you are. Okay, honey, have a great rest of the week, and we'll see you soon."

"Bye, Mom!" Putting down the phone, Andi felt a brief wave of homesickness wash over her. She forced her thoughts back to everything she'd done today and felt a little better. Dezba, Nascha, and Yas had been totally adorable. If she couldn't be with Buddy this week, the kittens would make great substitute pets. Plus she was still trying to furnish her new room. Where better to spend her time than the craft store? Washing her hands at the bathroom sink, Andi decided to call Nina and arrange to visit the Nelsons the next day.

As soon as she was awake the following morning, Andi rushed onto the deck to check her furniture.

"The paint has dried enough," said her dad, joining her. "We'll move it back to your room after breakfast."

Andi wolfed down a bowl of cereal and helped carry the bedframe back into her room. Her dad had been right. The color looked amazing against the red tiles.

"I'll get a yellow blanket to put on my bed," Andi decided. "And a yellow cushion for the chair. And I'm going to get a cactus for the corner of the room today."

"Let's get a horse and a billycan for good measure, and a couple of spittoons, for that authentic cowboy atmosphere," her dad joked. "Are you going back to the Nelsons' store today?"

"I'm heading over first thing," Andi said. When she called the previous night, Nina had invited her to help give the kittens their breakfast. "Can I borrow your camera? I want to take some pictures of the kittens to send to Trist and Nat."

Her dad reached for his car keys. "Sure. I'll drive you over."

"I know you've got work to do this morning," Andi said. "I thought I'd run, if that's okay with you." Andi spent a lot of her free time on the track in Orchard Park, training for the school track team. With no Buddy to walk, no bike to ride, and her dad driving everywhere, Andi's muscles were screaming for exercise.

"Run!" her dad sounded incredulous. "Are you sure? It must be a couple of miles."

"It's no farther than I run back home," Andi said, shrugging on a track top and tightening her sneakers. "I'll call you if I buy anything and need a ride back. What's the problem?" she added, noticing that her dad was staring at her.

"I guess I'm not used to you being so independent," he said. "I still think of you as a little kid. I don't know where the time has gone."

Andi kissed him goodbye, slung the camera around her shoulder, picked up a key, and let herself out of the condo. The air was warm, with a gentle breeze. She was soon running along the sidewalk with her arms pumping smoothly by her sides. Her legs felt like steel springs powering her down the street, and Andi imagined that if she lifted her feet any higher, she would be flying!

She arrived at Santa Rosa Crafts just as her breathing started getting a little ragged. Leaning down with her hands on her knees, Andi concentrated on getting her breath back. Tate was sitting in his usual place, with his eyes closed in the bright morning light.

"Where's the fire?" Nina stood smiling in the doorway of the store.

"No fire, just exercise," Andi panted. "Hi, Nina. How are the kittens?"

"Hungry." Nina held the door so Andi could follow her inside. "Dezba's tried to open the refrigerator already."

Mr. Nelson was adding some change to the cash register. "Good morning, Andi of the clan of O'Keefe," he said. "Are you taking the kittens off my hands today?"

"No, but I might buy a rug," Andi said. "Could you show me some more later on, Mr. Nelson?"

"With pleasure," replied the old man. "Now hurry and feed those cats before they destroy my kitchen."

The kittens were playing a crazy game of chase underneath the kitchen table. After giving them their food (and making sure Dezba didn't boss the others too much), Andi picked up Yas to stroke his tummy. With his deep throaty purr, Yas was fast becoming Andi's favorite — although doe-eyed Nascha and feisty Dezba were adorable as well.

"Nina!" Mr. Nelson called. "Can you come out here?"

Nina and Andi went back into the store closely followed by the kittens, who sniffed at the rugs and pounced on any loose threads they could see.

"Nina!" Dakota Nelson sighed. "Why can't you leave the kittens in the kitchen like I ask you?"

"I can't look after the store and the kittens unless they're both in the same place, Grandfather!" Nina protested. "They'll go to sleep soon, I promise."

The wind chimes tinkled and they turned to see a middle-aged couple in shorts and T-shirts standing in the doorway.

"What a lovely shop," the woman said enthusiastically. She had short brown hair with streaks of gray, and a camera was slung around her neck. She turned to her husband. "Don't you think so, Jim? I could buy everything in here, I really could."

Her husband, who wore a canvas baseball cap and had on white socks under his brown leather sandals, looked a little worried. "Not everything, Jane, dear," he said. "We couldn't fit it in the motor home."

"Take a look around and let me know if I can help you with anything," Mr. Nelson said with a smile. "Are those British accents, by the way?"

"That's right. We're Jim and Jane Tatford, from the county of Hampshire in the south of England. How d'you do?" Jim Tatford shook Mr. Nelson's hand and nodded at Andi and Nina.

"Are you on vacation in Arizona?" said Nina.

"Rather an extended holiday, actually," Jane Tatford

said. "We've hired a motor home to celebrate our retirement and plan to tour as much of America as we can manage in the next twelve months. We started in Miami and hope to end up in Alaska."

"We're in Arizona to see Monument Valley and your famous saguaro cacti," Mr. Tatford explained. "We're heading to the Grand Canyon in a couple of days."

Jane Tatford was looking at the tree of life rug. "This carpet is exquisite," she exclaimed, leaning over to get a closer look. "Look at these pretty little birds!"

Andi listened while Mr. Nelson explained its significance, happy that the British woman appreciated it as much as she did.

Mrs. Tatford looked around for her husband. "What do you think, Jim?"

Mr. Tatford took off his hat and scratched his head. "It's fine, but it really is too big for us, Jane," he said. "We can't fill the motor home in our first two months! Why don't you choose something a little smaller?"

Although Andi knew the rug was too expensive for her budget, she was relieved that the Tatfords weren't going to buy it. She wanted it to stay in the store for at least as long as she was staying with her dad.

"Here's a gorgeous little piece of pottery," Mr. Tatford

said, studying a honey-colored vase painted with a ring of stylized feathers. "Look at this marvelous feather effect. It's like looking at the rays of the sun."

"That's a sandpainting vase," Mr. Nelson explained. "Sandpainting is sacred to the Navajo tradition. Our medicine men make images like this on the ground out of colored sand — red, white, blue, yellow — to perform healing ceremonies. When the ceremony is complete, they must destroy the painting. And they must destroy it in precisely the same order in which they make it, to avoid angering the gods."

"It's beautiful," Mr. Tatford murmured. "It's a salt glaze, isn't it? I wish I could get my glazes to look like that. I'm a keen potter myself — I have a wheel in the garden shed and a kiln in the garage. I'm no painter, though. Not like the chap who made this."

After some deliberation, the Tatfords came over to the cash register. Mr. Tatford was still holding the honey-colored pot, and Mrs. Tatford had picked up a pretty basket with a red-and-black stylized face woven into the lid. As they handed the items to Mr. Nelson, Nina suddenly flew over and snatched the basket out of their hands.

"No!" she cried. "Not that one!"

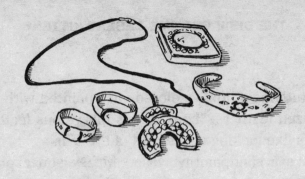

Chapter Five

"What on earth — " Mr. Tatford spluttered.

"Nina!" Mr. Nelson growled. "What is the meaning of this disrespect to our customers?"

Nina flushed. "I'm sorry, Grandfather, I didn't mean to be rude," she said, embarrassed. "It's just — the kittens are sleeping in this one."

Andi lifted the lid of the basket and everyone peered inside. Dezba, Yas, and Nascha blinked sleepily up at them.

"Oh, aren't they heavenly!" Mrs. Tatford said, reaching into the basket to pet the kittens. "What exquisite coloring! And look at the little brown one's eyes! I've never seen anything so beautiful."

Nascha opened her mouth and gave a tiny mew, then snuggled back down beside her brother and sister.

Andi could see that Mr. Nelson was still angry. "Nina, I

told you to get rid of those cats. I can't have them disturbing the customers," he said with a frown.

Mrs. Tatford looked worried. "Get rid of them? Oh no! They aren't disturbing us. In fact, they've made our day, haven't they, Jim? We adore cats," she explained. "Our beloved Sooty died not so long ago, and we miss him terribly. He had a good, long life, but nothing can replace that feeling of him curled up on my lap on a dark evening." Mrs. Tatford looked sad, then brightened up again as she stroked Dezba between the ears.

"They *are* very pretty," Jim Tatford agreed. "Where is their mother?"

"We don't know," Nina told them. "She disappeared."

"That's awful!" Mr. Tatford exclaimed. "Will she come back?"

Nina stroked Yas's tiny paws, and the little cat flexed his claws at her. "We hope so," she said. "But she's half wild. Feral cats are very unpredictable."

"We haven't seen any stray cats around here," Mrs. Tatford commented.

"You don't see them very often," Nina said matter-of-factly. "They get eaten by coyotes."

The Tatfords gasped.

"Coyotes!" Andi was shocked, too. "That's horrible!"

"I know," Nina agreed. "But that's desert life for you.

Oh, I'm sure Mosi, their mother, is all right," she added, seeing the expressions on their faces. "She's pretty clever. She's been around for a few years and knows the dangers. She'll come back, eventually."

Mrs. Tatford was appalled. "But her poor kittens! What's going to happen to them?"

"They'll be fine," Nina reassured the British woman. "We can't keep them in the store forever, but — "

Suddenly Dezba made a leap out of the basket. It was a long way down to the floor, but the little tabby landed neatly on her four paws and took off toward the door. Andi raced after her, reaching the door just in time to shut it. The noise from the traffic outside immediately died. Dezba narrowed her green eyes and made a dash for the window, scrambling up on a pile of rugs by digging her claws into the wool.

"My rugs!" Mr. Nelson shouted. "Those cats will ruin them!"

Dezba bunched her haunches and sprang away from Andi's outstretched hands and around the walls of the store, jumping from one rail to the next in a whirl of tabby fur.

Nina put the other kittens down and hurried to help Andi. Dezba had vanished beneath a display cabinet again. This time she wasn't falling for Andi's dangling cord routine, and refused to come out.

"I hate to say it, but the other two have gotten out of the basket now," Mr. Tatford pointed out, as Yas and Nascha tumbled happily across the floor.

Mr. Nelson sighed and scooped up the wriggling kittens. Then he marched through to the back of the store and put them in the kitchen. "When you catch Dezba, she can join the others," he told Nina and Andi, who were lying on their stomachs peering under the cabinet. "I won't have them in my store if they continue to make this much trouble, Nina — do you understand me?" He turned to the Tatfords, who were waiting patiently by the register with a different basket. "I'm sorry. Kittens never do as they are told — and neither do granddaughters. Allow me to wrap those for you."

Andi made a lightning-quick grab underneath the cabinet. "Gotcha!" she declared in triumph, pulling Dezba out by the scruff of her neck. Bringing the kitten up so she was level with her face, Andi tapped her gently on the nose. "If you escape one more time, we won't be responsible for you," she warned Dezba. "The coyotes will get you, and that will be that!"

Dezba blinked at Andi and twitched her ears.

"She won't listen to you," Nina sighed, following Andi

through to the kitchen where she placed Dezba next to her siblings in a cardboard box underneath the table.

"I know," Andi replied with a wry smile. "But there's no harm in trying."

When they came out of the kitchen, the Tatfords had gone. Mr. Nelson was standing with his arms folded and a face like thunder.

Nina raised her hands. "Don't say anything, Grandfather," she begged. "I know. This is a store, not a zoo. I'm sorry, and I promise it won't happen again."

Mr. Nelson's expression softened. "If you are truly sorry, Nina, you can help me polish the jewelry this morning."

The jewelry in the display cases was beautiful, but it was very intricate and looked difficult to clean.

"I'll help, too," Andi offered.

"Thank you." Nina's grandfather was looking less annoyed with every moment. "We'll start now, while the store is quiet. Then you can play with those kittens again, if you must."

"Yes, Grandfather," Nina said humbly, but she winked at Andi to show that she knew they weren't really being punished.

They set to work with the polishing cloths, and Andi asked Nina lots of questions about the trail ride they were going on the following day. The ponies and the scenery sounded amazing, and made for great conversation while their hands were busy with the jewelry. The silver cuffs, coral and jet and agate pendants, silver belt buckles, turquoise rings, and shell chokers were exquisite, and polishing them was a pleasure, not a chore. There was one beautiful necklace of silver and turquoise that Andi particularly liked, and she took extra care with each link and curve.

"That is a traditional squash blossom necklace," Nina explained. "See this curved *naja*? That means 'pendant', by the way." She pointed to the horseshoe-shape dangling from the bottom of the necklace. "The People learned silversmithing from the Mexicans many years ago. This pattern was based on the pomegranate flower, which the Spanish settlers often wore on their clothing."

"So it's a pomegranate flower, not a squash blossom?" Andi asked, frowning.

Nina laughed. "It's both," she said. "When the style developed, the People had never seen a pomegranate, and they thought it looked like one of our native flowers, the squash blossom."

Toward the end of the day, Andi called her dad to get a ride home. When he came to pick her up, she dragged him to the back of the store to show him a blanket that she'd found.

"It would to be perfect for my bed!" she said. "And guess what? It's on sale!"

"Glad to see you're being sensible about your purchases," Mr. Talbot said approvingly.

Andi thought of the tree of life rug. It was hard to be sensible where that was concerned.

"Dad," she asked, "can Nina come back for dinner tonight? We've got stuff to plan for tomorrow's trail ride."

Mr. Talbot nodded. "Sure, if it's okay with her folks. It'll be a pleasure to have you, Nina." He glanced around the store. "So where are the kittens, then? Don't tell me you've lost them, Andi. I thought you were a pet finder, not a pet *loser*."

Nina looked surprised. "Do you really find pets for people, Andi?"

"My daughter is famous for it, apparently," Mr. Talbot said with a smile. "Didn't the White House call you a while back about a missing cat?"

Andi swallowed her irritation. "Real funny, Dad," she said. "I set up the Pet Finders Club with my friends Tristan and Natalie," she explained to Nina.

"That's cool!" Nina said, sounding impressed. "How many animals have you found?"

"So many!" Andi said. "Once we found the contents of a whole pet store."

"No wonder you were so good at getting Dezba out from under that cabinet," Nina said. "What a great idea to set up a club to help people who've lost pets!"

How come Nina understands that, but not my own dad? Andi thought unhappily.

Nina agreed to come over around six-thirty for dinner. Back at the condo, Andi and her dad began applying second coats to Andi's desk and chair. But the wind was picking up and dust was beginning to swirl around the deck and stick to the wet paint, so they abandoned it eventually. While her dad got them something to drink, Andi went to her room and logged on to the computer, which was sitting on the floor underneath the window. There was an e-mail from Natalie waiting for her.

Howdy, Arizonian!
I'm sitting in my room wearing my scarf and thickest sweater. It's so cold here the wind freezes your nose hairs! And it hasn't even snowed yet! Jet refuses to sit at my feet, even though I've tried the 'sit' command lots of times.

We're doing walking to heel in the obedience class now, but I can't get Jet anywhere near my feet. Maybe my new red boots are scaring him away. Have you got a tan yet?

Sprawling flat on her stomach, Andi tapped out a reply.

I'm wearing shorts and a T-shirt, ha ha! It's cold here at night, and the wind is sometimes a little gritty from the desert, but it's pretty nice for December. Dad and I have been on the deck, painting my new furniture. You'd really like the color (bright blue), and I bet you would totally want a tank top in the exact same shade.

I've made friends with this girl named Nina whose grand-father owns a craft store — and she's got three kittens! They're totally adorable. Dezba's the naughty one, Nascha is the pretty one, and Yas is just a total cutie. I'm attaching a picture that I took today with my dad's camera. They love hanging out in the store, which must seem like a big play-ground to them — baskets to hide in, rugs to sharpen their claws on, dangling jewelry to bat at with their paws. Nina's grandfather doesn't like them too much, though.

Andi finished off with a description of the things she had bought for her room and pressed the send button. Her e-mail flew satisfyingly off the screen, and she smiled as she pictured Natalie reading it under layers and layers of winter clothes. Then she settled down to write to her mom and Tristan.

The wind died down in the afternoon, so Andi and her dad went back to painting the furniture. Andi had just finished the second coat when the light faded and she and her dad had to pack up their brushes. Andi took a long hot shower, enjoying the sensation of the water pounding on her aching muscles as it washed away a tide of blue paint from her skin.

When she came out of the shower, she found Nina in the living room, talking to her dad.

"There you are! I thought we were going to have to send a search party for you," Mr. Talbot joked. "Nina's been waiting for you for fifteen minutes."

"I know I'm kind of early for dinner, but I just had to come tell you," Nina said. "You know the trail ride we were going on tomorrow?"

Andi looked at her in dismay. "Don't tell me it's been canceled?"

"In a way." Nina's eyes gleamed. "My grandfather wants to take us to the Canyon de Chelly, instead!"

Andi was puzzled. "Where's that?"

"It's a sacred site of the People," Nina explained. "The

Navajo have lived there for hundreds of years. Very few tourists can go there, and there are parts of the canyon that you can only visit if you are with a Navajo guide. It's a three-hour drive, so we're going to stay overnight at the canyon with some members of Grandfather's clan who live there. It's a really special place, Andi. Your dad already said you can come with us, and I just know you're going to love it!"

Chapter Six

Andi leaped out of bed as soon as the sun peeped over the mountains the following morning. She dressed carefully — a white-and-blue checked shirt, jeans, and boots — and packed everything she was going to need for her overnight stay, including her dad's digital camera, which he had agreed to lend her for the trip. Last of all, she packed the dark leather riding chaps she'd bought back home for the lessons she'd taken at Hollow Creek.

"Take them," her mom had advised. "They ride horses in Arizona, and knowing you and animals, you're bound to get a chance to use them." *You were so right, Mom!* Andi thought happily, zipping up her bag and cramming a red baseball cap on her head.

Her dad drove her over to Santa Rosa Crafts, where Nina and her grandfather were waiting beside an old pickup truck that was attached to a two-horse trailer. Andi slung her bag in the back of the pickup and scrambled into the cab beside Nina.

"Don't mind old Tate," Mr. Nelson said, reaching over to pat the old hunting dog who was sitting on the floor. "He's older than you two, so he's entitled to take up a little extra space."

Tate whined a greeting and settled his large head on Andi's knee. Andi pet him and leaned back in the worn leather seat with a sigh of satisfaction.

"We're going to pick up our horses at the trail-riding center," Nina explained as they drove out of town. "I usually ride Raven. He's a gorgeous black quarter horse with the sweetest temper you ever saw. I think my mom will give you Kai. She's a dream to ride — you'll love her."

"Is Kai a Navajo name, like the kittens?" Andi asked, scratching Tate between the ears until the old dog groaned with pleasure.

"Yup, it means willow tree," Nina explained. "She's a palomino, which is a kind of golden creamy color. We can't take a horse for Grandfather because we only have a two-horse trailer, but he likes to borrow his brother's gelding, Cisco, up at the canyon."

"His brother?" Andi echoed. "So your great-uncle lives at the canyon?"

"Actually, no. Clifford's not my grandfather's brother in the American sense," Nina said. "You'd say he was a cousin. The way of the People is to call everyone 'brother' or 'sister' if you are in the same clan. If you meet people who are much older than you, then you maybe call them 'aunt' or 'grandfather'."

Andi made a face. "That sounds really confusing."

"It's easy, once you get used to it," Nina said.

Nina's mom, Angie, was waiting for them in the yard at the riding center. She looked just like Nina, with the same long dark hair and wide smile. She wore a velvet blouse and faded jeans over battered suede boots, with several turquoise and coral necklaces around her neck. "I feel like I know you already," she said, giving Andi a warm hug. "Nina's been talking about you nonstop. Your pet-finding business sounds terrific."

As Nina had predicted, Angie had Raven and Kai waiting for them. Feeling like this was turning into one of the best days ever, Andi stroked Kai's sand-colored nose and admired her contrasting white-blond mane, while Nina fed Raven mints and stroked him under his whiskery chin.

"I'll look after the store until you get back," Angie promised Nina's grandfather. "Two Clouds will take care of things here for me."

"Who's Two Clouds?" Andi asked Nina.

"He's my youngest uncle, in both the American sense and the Navajo one," Nina replied. "You'd like him — he's fun."

"It must be great to have your family around you all the time," Andi said a little wistfully. "I don't have any relatives living near me, apart from my mom."

"It's okay," Nina said. "But it can get old sometimes. Your whole family knows everything about you — nothing is private."

Andi pondered this as they loaded the horses and said good-bye to Angie, who handed them a bag of home-baked oatmeal cookies for the journey. Andi decided it would be worth losing a little privacy to have such a nice family nearby.

They drove down a dusty gray road for what felt like several hundred miles, stopping off every hour to give the horses water. Tate occasionally climbed out to drink some water, but generally stayed in the cab with his head resting either on his paws or on Andi's knee.

"Tate's very quiet," Andi observed, scratching the old dog between the ears.

"He knows we're going to a sacred place," Nina said. "He's full of deep doggy thoughts. Aren't you, boy?"

Tate yawned and shifted his head slightly so that Andi could scratch him under the chin.

Nina asked her grandfather to turn on the radio, and she and Andi sang along at the top of their voices while Dakota rolled his eyes at the music. At last, the pickup slowed down and turned off the main road. Andi caught her breath. Straight ahead, the flat, featureless desert reared up into the sky to form towering cliffs of bright red stone. She leaned out of the pickup window to see better.

Mr. Nelson pulled up beside a small ranch house surrounded by a wooden fence. Three Navajo men were waiting by the gate.

"*Yatahey*, Clifford." Nina's grandfather climbed out of the cab and embraced a man in a big black Stetson hat. "It's been a long time, brother. How are you?"

Clifford smiled, revealing several missing teeth. "Good, Dakota. Nina, you've grown! And who is your friend?"

Nina introduced Andi to Clifford. Billy and Chee, the other men with Clifford, nodded and smiled in greeting, their silver belt buckles gleaming in the sunlight.

"My wife has prepared some lunch for us," Clifford told them. "Afterward, Dakota will take you through the canyon to the village, where you'll spend the night."

Andi and Nina helped Billy and Chee unload the horses and tie them to a rail in an open-sided barn. There was a lively paint gelding tied to the rail as well, which snorted and tossed its mane when Andi reached out a hand to stroke its velvety nose.

"That's Cisco," Nina explained. "Grandfather always rides him when we come out here."

They followed the men into the ranch. An appetizing smell wafted out on the warm desert air and Andi's mouth watered. They'd been driving for so long, she could barely remember having breakfast.

Clifford's wife, Happy, was small and bright-eyed like a bird, busily ladling out bowlfuls of lamb stew and handing them around the wooden table. Bright rugs hung on the walls, bringing flashes of color into the room. Andi counted eight people around the table — herself, Nina, Mr. Nelson, Clifford, Happy, Billy, Chee, and an old woman who sat quietly in the corner. Her gray hair was wound up in a tight bun. She was introduced as Happy's mother, Clara.

"Why doesn't Clifford like Happy's mother?" Andi whispered to Nina when they went outside to saddle Kai and Raven.

Nina looked surprised. "Why do you say that?"

"He didn't look at her once during the meal," Andi said.

Nina roared with laughter. "Clifford likes to keep the old ways," she said, "and it's considered taboo to look at your wife's mother."

"He never looks at her?" Andi said incredulously, tightening Kai's girth the way she'd been taught at Hollow Creek. "But she lives in his house!"

"It's the tradition," Nina said with a shrug. She swung herself onto Raven's back and rested her feet in the stirrups. The small, powerful horse gave a snort and tossed his jet-black mane.

"Hurry up, you two," Mr. Nelson said, leading Cisco out of the barn. He'd saddled the gelding so deftly that Andi had barely noticed. "Let's get going."

Andi looked back at the house. "Isn't Tate coming with us?"

"He's too old for long trips into the canyon these days," Mr. Nelson replied. "Happy lit a fire, so he'll have a great time dozing in front of it. We'll see him tomorrow."

Cisco scraped the dusty ground with his front hoof. Andi admired the way Mr. Nelson kept the restless horse in check, holding the reins lightly in one hand and

steering the gelding with his knees. She really appreciated the lessons she'd had at Hollow Creek, because
Nina and her grandfather were obviously very experi-
enced riders. Bending forward, she ran her hand down
Kai's mane and silently asked her to take care of them
both on the uneven ground. Kai jerked her head, making
the bit rattle, as if she was promising to do her best.

They set off, falling into single file down a narrow
path where the bright red rock loomed high on either
side. For the first time since her conversation with Tristan, Andi wondered if she'd really see a rattlesnake. A
snake had spooked her pony on her first ride at Hollow
Creek, and she didn't want the same thing to happen
with Kai.

When they reached a flat green plateau sliced in two
by a river, Mr. Nelson began to tell the legend of the
Navajo.

"The People came from three different underworlds
and emerged into this fourth world, the Glittering
World, through a cornstalk," he began. "First Man was
made in the east, from the meeting of the white and
black clouds. First Woman was made in the west, from
the joining of the yellow and blue clouds. They arranged
our land within the protection of the four sacred mountains to the north, south, east, and west. The mountains

each contained the four sacred stones — abalone, coral, white shell, and black jet. . . . ”

Andi's head filled with glittering images of gods, mountains, and monsters as they left the valley and headed up toward the barren rocks. Suddenly, her attention was drawn to the cliff face. Tucked beneath a vast overhang of rock, she could see what looked like a neat stone and adobe-brick village. She pointed it out to Nina.

“Is that where we're spending the night?” she asked.

Nina grinned. “Not unless you want to sleep with the spirits of the Ancient Ones,” she said. “The Ancients left the canyon more than seven hundred years ago, two hundred years before the People came to this place.”

Andi stared at the buildings. They looked perfect, barely damaged at all, even though they had been empty for so long. “Why did they leave?”

“They ran out of water,” Mr. Nelson said simply. “This is a hard land, Andi.”

Andi imagined the village buildings once bustling with life and felt sad.

As they moved higher up the canyon toward the deserted village, Andi saw birds, snakes, and strange dancing figures carved into the bleached rock. Most eerily of all, she saw the ghostly red outlines of hand-prints.

"Is this village haunted?" she asked uneasily.

Nina shook her head. "There are spirits in parts of the Canyon del Muerto, north of here," she said. "Many Navajo died there, betrayed by one of their own people during a war. It isn't a place that I like to visit."

Nina's words sent shivers down Andi's spine, and she urged Kai faster along the track.

The canyon grew more magnificent with each turn of the trail. Vast stacks of rock reached up into the sky like fingers, while the cliffs looked like someone had piled up hundreds of paper-thin pancakes in every color, from palest ivory to a deep burgundy. More abandoned buildings were revealed around every corner, crouched under crags and overhangs of rock. The riders passed orchards of gnarled, stunted trees and watered the horses at glittering creeks and waterfalls. The canyon was like a perfect, hidden world.

"I could stay out here forever," Andi sighed, as the setting sun made the rocks glow like molten copper. "If the weather stayed like this, I don't think I'd ever go indoors!"

"You would be in good company," Mr. Nelson said. "The People believe that if they die out in the open, their spirits are free and they can dwell in the land and sky forever."

Up ahead, Andi saw the flickering fires of a village. Unlike the abandoned village of the Ancients, this village stood away from the rocks and overhangs and buzzed with activity. Several round mud houses with wooden doorways were scattered around a creek, smoke rising from holes set into their roofs. A campfire blazed on a patch of open ground and the villagers were gathered around it, talking and eating.

"You've come at a lucky time," Dakota said to Andi. "The villagers usually leave the canyon in the winter, but it's been mild enough to stay this year."

As they rode up to the village, the people got to their feet to welcome them. Three dogs came running out of one of the houses, barking furiously, and Mr. Nelson knelt down and played with them until they squirmed happily in the dust by his feet. It reminded Andi of the way Nina's grandfather had been with Tate, back at Santa Rosa Crafts.

As soon as the horses were untacked and hitched to rails, steaming bowls of food were pressed into the visitors' hands and they were ushered over to the fire. Andi ate the hot hash and beans gratefully. All this fresh air had given her an appetite to rival even Tristan's!

"This is Yazzie." Mr. Nelson introduced Andi to an older man who wore a red bandana around his grizzled head. Several heavy turquoise and coral rings decorated his gnarled fingers. "He's the village elder and medicine man. Yazzie's lived here all his life."

Yazzie smiled, one of his teeth glinting gold in the setting sun. His face was a map of lines and wrinkles, and his gray hair curled around his shoulders. He held Andi's gaze steadily, and Andi felt a strong sense of something wise and ancient in his eyes. It was easy to imagine him conducting a healing ceremony with a sandpainting like the one Mr. Nelson had described to the Tatfords.

After supper, Andi sat wide-eyed, listening to the soothing flow of chatter, laughter, and songs, and watching the flickering shadows on the mud houses and the canyon walls. Yazzie didn't speak much English, but as the fire died down and the villagers began to head to their individual houses, he beckoned Andi and Nina over to one of the huts to show them where they would sleep. The wooden door was so low that Andi had to duck to get through. Inside there was a pair of bunk beds piled high with red-and-yellow blankets. A hand loom leaned against one mud wall, displaying a half-finished rug in the same colors of wool.

Andi washed her face in a bowl of water set on the floor and collapsed gratefully on her bed. Nina went to shut the wooden door.

"Oh, don't shut the door yet," Andi begged. "I can see the stars from my bunk. I've never seen them so bright."

"There is a Navajo story about the night sky," Nina said, climbing into the bunk above Andi. "In the new Glittering World, the People had arranged the mountains, the sun, and the moon exactly as they wanted them. Then they tried to decide how to arrange the stars. But before they could make a decision, the Coyote — he's the trickster of many Navajo stories — came and stole the stars and scattered them at random, all across the sky."

Andi smiled as she stared up at the burning stars. They were as sharp and bright as diamonds. "Random is good," she said and closed her eyes.

In the gray light of morning, Andi, Nina, and Mr. Nelson saddled the horses and shook hands with the villagers, who crowded around them to say good-bye. Yazzie's hand was strong and hard, like weathered oak. He smiled and said something to Andi in Navajo.

"Yazzie says that you have a strong spirit," Nina said.

She sounded impressed. "He doesn't say that about many people."

Andi felt very proud. She beamed at Yazzie, hoping he understood how pleased she was by his compliment. She really hoped she could come back to this special place some day, maybe to show it to her dad. As she thanked the villagers for their hospitality, she tried to fix every detail of the scene in her mind: the smell of the baked earth and the fire smoke, the colors of the villagers' clothes, the feel of their handwoven blankets, and the warmth of their welcome. She knew it was an experience she would remember forever.

Mr. Nelson led them back to Clifford and Happy's ranch by a different route, one high above the rushing river. The views were breathtaking, stretching far across the canyon, with the river running like a thin brown thread below. Andi felt as if they were journeying forward through time, returning to the modern world that had seemed so far away while they were in the Navajo village.

Back at the ranch, Tate thumped his tail on the hearth rug in greeting.

"He hasn't moved from the fire since you left," Happy told them.

"Very sensible, at his age," Mr. Nelson said as Tate slowly got to his paws and walked across the room to press his nose into his master's hand. "You missed nothing you haven't seen before, old friend."

They loaded the horses into the trailer and stowed their bags, then said goodbye to Clifford and his family. Andi rested her hands on the back of the cab seat, watching through the rear window as the great cliffs of the Canyon de Chelly faded into the distance. She couldn't wait to upload the pictures she'd taken on her dad's camera, and she decided that, if any of the pictures were good enough, she was going to get them enlarged and framed to hang on the walls of her new room.

They took Kai and Raven back to the trail-riding center, where Andi met Nina's uncle Two Clouds. He was eager to hear about their trip, and it was obvious he felt a strong connection to the place where his ancestors had lived for hundreds of years. Then they piled back into the pickup and headed back to Santa Rosa Crafts.

"We're back!" Mr. Nelson called, putting the bags down by the cash register. "Angie, are you here?"

Andi looked around for the kittens. She was dying to pick them up and cuddle them.

Nina was obviously feeling the same way. "Mom?" she asked, as Angie came out of the kitchen drying her hands. "Where are the kittens?"

"Welcome back, " Angie smiled. "Haven't seen the kittens since lunch. They're probably asleep somewhere."

Nina paused. "Since lunch?" she echoed. "But it's five o'clock, Mom. You mean you haven't seen them all afternoon?"

Angie frowned. "No. Should I have?"

"Didn't you feed them at three?" Nina was beginning to look anxious.

"I put out their food, yes," Angie said. Now she was looking worried, too.

Nina hurried to the kitchen and checked the food bowls. Then she turned around and stared in horror at Andi. "Their food is still there," she said. "They always eat it — every last scrap. I think . . . I think they're gone!"

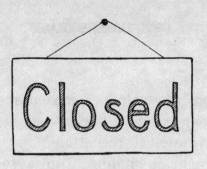

Chapter Seven

"Gone?" Andi cried. Finding animals in Orchard Park was one thing, but Tucson? It was about six times as big for a start, and she barely knew ten blocks of it. And the kittens were so tiny! Thoughts of hungry coyotes loomed terrifyingly in her mind.

"Andi, you're good at finding pets." Nina grasped Andi's arm. "What should we do?"

Andi pulled herself together. Suddenly, she wasn't tired any more. Her pet-finding instincts were already kicking in. First, they needed to pinpoint exactly when the kittens disappeared. She searched through her bag for a pen and paper. *If Tristan were here,* she thought regretfully, *he'd have one of his red notebooks to keep track of the investigation.* But the other pet finders were hundreds of miles away, and Andi was on her own.

"Mrs. Nelson," she said in her calmest, most professional voice. "Please think back. When is the last time that you're sure you saw the kittens?"

"Just before lunch, I think," Angie said, frowning. "Yes — they went to sleep in one of the baskets about one o'clock. I remember noticing when I went out back to grab something to eat."

"Could they have gone out the door when you weren't looking?" Mr. Nelson asked.

Angie shook her head. "I kept the door closed all day because the wind kept blowing dust into the store. I spent half the afternoon sweeping the floor and shaking the rugs."

Andi made a note. "What about when customers came in and out? You said the store was busy today."

Angie looked worried. "Would they really go out in the street on their own?"

"They have been getting more adventurous," Nina said, white with anxiety. "Especially Dezba. If she got outside, the others would have followed her."

"Oh, this is awful!" Angie was close to tears. "You leave me in charge for one day and this happens. Nina, I'm so sorry."

Nina patted her mom on the shoulder. "It's okay," she

said. "Andi finds pets back home all the time. She's practically a professional."

Andi smiled at Nina. "Thanks for the vote of confidence," she said, trying not to let her worry show in her voice. "First, let's divide the store up and search it. If they're still inside, that'll be the quickest way to find them."

Nina's mom and grandfather went to look upstairs while Andi and Nina turned the sign on the door to CLOSED and searched every inch of the store. They looked underneath each cabinet, turned all the baskets and pots upside down, and peered inside every rolled-up carpet. Andi went through the stock in the window as well, and Nina emptied the cupboards in the kitchen. They hunted in drawers, behind wall hangings — they even opened the jewelry cabinets. But the kittens were nowhere to be found.

"Well, this is a hive of industry." Mr. Talbot stood in the doorway gazing at Andi and Nina, who were on their knees among piles of baskets, rugs, and pots. "I came to take you home, Andi, but it looks like you're pretty busy. Did you have a good trip?"

"Dad!" Andi scrambled to her feet and ran over to him. "The trip was great, but I'll tell you about that later.

The kittens have disappeared! Can you close the door behind you? Just in case they're in here somewhere and try to get out."

Mr. Talbot looked taken aback. "Yes ma'am," he said, shutting the door. "Do you want to search me as well?" He pulled his pockets inside out and held his arms out to the side.

Andi felt impatient. "Dad, this is no joke. Help us look, will you?"

"Of course," her dad said hastily. "Where should I start?"

"We've covered pretty much everywhere except the top shelves over there," Andi said, pointing. "Even with the stepladder, Nina and I aren't tall enough to search them. You're tall, Dad — can you reach them?"

Mr. Talbot pulled a stepladder toward him and climbed up to examine the shelves. "You seem to know what you're doing," he remarked, hunting through the neatly stacked baskets. "I wouldn't have thought of looking up here."

"I've had a lot of practice finding pets, remember?" Andi said. She waited for her dad to come back with one of his joking replies. But he just nodded and turned to the next stack of baskets.

They continued hunting for another hour, carefully

searching their designated areas but finding nothing.

"Anything upstairs?" Nina demanded when Angie and Dakota Nelson returned.

Mr. Nelson shook his head. "Nothing," he said heavily. For all his complaints about the kittens in the store, it looked like, deep down, he was as fond of them as Nina and Andi were.

Andi looked around for Tate. The old hunting dog was sleeping on a blanket at the back of the store. "If we gave Tate one of the baskets the kittens used to sleep in, do you think he'd be able to use his nose to help us find them?"

Mr. Nelson looked uncertain. "His sense of smell isn't what it used to be, but we can give it a try," he said. "Tate, boy, come!"

Tate heaved himself to his paws and padded over. Mr. Nelson showed him the red-and-gold basket Andi remembered seeing the kittens in the very first time she visited the store. Tate sniffed at it, blinked up at Mr. Nelson, and then ambled back to his blanket, where he collapsed with a sigh.

Mr. Nelson shrugged apologetically. "I guess he's not a hunter anymore," he said. "I did warn you."

Andi stifled a yawn, suddenly feeling dog tired herself.

"Listen," Mr. Talbot said, checking his watch. "It's getting pretty late and you've had a long day. We should call it a night."

"But Dad—" Andi started to protest.

"No, Andi," said her dad, sounding firm. "I know from experience that you can't do a good job when you can't keep your eyes open."

"The same goes for you, Nina," Angie Nelson said gently. "We've done the best we can tonight. We'll keep looking in the morning."

Nina's eyes filled with tears. "But the kittens are too young to be out on their own all night without their mom!"

Mr. Nelson put his arm around Nina's shoulders. "Dezba will keep them all together," he said. "She's got the makings of a fierce little mother herself. Don't worry, Nina. Everything will be okay."

As soon as they got back to her dad's condo, Andi logged on to the computer and sent an e-mail to Tristan and Natalie. They might have been hundreds of miles away, but she needed their help.

SOS!
The kittens are missing! We've searched the store and the apartment upstairs, but there's no sign of them.

She tapped out a few more details about the store and sent the e-mail. Then she sat and stared at the blank screen, gnawing at her thumbnail while she waited hopefully for a reply. There was no response. Sighing, Andi got ready for bed. Sleep took a long time to come.

The first finger of light had barely peeped through the drapes before Andi was back sitting at her computer. There were two responses waiting for her.

Andi,
Sorry about the kittens. Have you tried the local animal shelter? Someone may have found them and turned them in. If the three of them stuck together like you think, they would have been pretty noticeable out on the street. And I don't want to worry you, but remember — Tucson is major snake country, and the kittens could end up as reptile food if you don't find them soon.
See ya (wouldn't want to be ya),
Tristan

"Great," Andi muttered to herself. "First coyotes, now snakes." Trying not to think about all the dangers lurking in the desert, she jotted down Tristan's idea about the shelter. She'd check out her dad's phonebooks as soon as she'd read Natalie's e-mail.

Hi Andi,
Nat here! Listen — I checked your last e-mail and you mentioned how you first saw the kittens in a basket in the store. I wondered if maybe someone could have bought a basket with the kittens inside, by mistake? Is that a dumb idea?

Andi stared at the screen. "Nat, you're a *genius*!" Nina's mom had said that the kittens fell asleep in a basket just before lunch. They could easily have stayed asleep most of the afternoon, and someone could just as easily have bought them. Nina's mom had been very busy yesterday. She might have forgotten to check the baskets she was selling. That British couple had almost bought a basket containing the kittens the other day, now that Andi stopped to think about it.

She pulled on some clothes and ran into the living area. "Dad!" she called. "Can you give me a ride to Santa Rosa Crafts, like, *now*?"

Her dad appeared at the bathroom door, his face half

covered with shaving foam. "Let me finish shaving first," he protested, waving his razor. "I can't show up to work with half a mustache."

Andi waited impatiently for her dad to finish, then dashed into the bathroom to brush her teeth and splash some cold water on her face. She pulled on her sneakers and grabbed her bag and her dad's camera with one hand and a piece of toast with the other.

"Hurry, Dad," she begged, as Mr. Talbot steered his Jeep onto the road heading into town.

They reached Santa Rosa Crafts ten minutes later. Barely stopping to wave good-bye to her dad, Andi sprinted into the store and looked around. "Nina!" she called. "Mr. Nelson? Mrs. Nelson? Anyone here?"

Nina pushed through the beaded curtain at the back of the store. She had a box of cat food in her hand, and she looked as if she hadn't slept all night.

Andi looked at the food. Hope soared in her heart. "Did you find them? Where are they? Are you giving them breakfast?"

"No, I don't know, and no, again," Nina said wearily. "I've been up since dawn, shaking this box. They usually come running when they hear it. But not this time. Oh Andi, what are we going to do?"

"Listen," Andi said urgently. "My friend Natalie had a great idea. . . . " She told Nina what Nat had suggested about the baskets.

Nina went pale. "But if they were sold in a basket, we'll *never* find them!"

"We will if your mom kept a record of what she sold yesterday," Andi assured her. "We can trace people that way. Maybe your mom can remember which basket she saw the kittens sleeping in?"

"I'm sorry, but I can't," Angie Nelson said, overhearing them. "But I do remember selling a couple of baskets yesterday. I guess I can check the receipts."

"Good," Andi said. "I have a backup plan as well. My friend Tristan suggested that we go check out the local animal shelter. I should have thought of that right away. Is there a shelter nearby?"

"The closest one's a couple of blocks away," Nina told her. "Mom, can we head over there right now?"

"Sure," Angie Nelson agreed. She was already checking through the previous day's receipts, which she had taken out of the cash register. "Maybe I'll have some information for you by the time you get back."

Andi and Nina ran all the way to the shelter, which was tucked down a dusty side street and had cheerful, sun-faded posters of dogs and cats pinned up in the windows. Inside, Andi saw a wall of kennels containing lost and stray animals to one side of the reception desk. There were several stocky dogs like Tate, a cockatoo with a pale pink crest and a missing claw, and three iguanas that were sitting motionless underneath a heater. But there were no cats to be seen. Andi couldn't help thinking nervously of coyotes again.

Ahyoka, the woman behind the reception desk, listened carefully as Andi explained what had happened. But to Andi's dismay, she shook her head.

"I wish I could tell you something different, but no one brought in any kittens yesterday," she said apologetically.

Nina's shoulders sagged. "Okay," she said. "It was worth a shot. Are there any other animal shelters in town that might be worth checking out?"

"There are several, but they're all quite a few miles away," said Ahyoka.

The kittens were unlikely to have traveled that far. Andi glanced at the bulletin board, which was dotted with posters of missing animals. They reminded her of all the posters she'd made with the Pet Finders Club back home.

Ahyoka saw her looking. "If you have a photograph of

the kittens, you could put together a poster on the shelter computer," she suggested. "I don't mind printing a few copies for you."

"We don't have any photos," Nina began, but Andi grabbed her arm.

"I have my dad's camera!" she said. "I took some pictures of the kittens a couple of days ago, remember?"

Due to the number of digital cameras the center used, Ahyoka told them, they luckily had the necessary software already installed on the computer. She showed them how to use it — it wasn't much different from Andi's mom's computer back home — and Andi was soon uploading photos and designing text.

"You make this look so easy," Nina said, watching Andi type in the Santa Rosa Crafts phone number. "I'm so glad you're here, Andi. I just wish I didn't have to use your pet-finding experience, if you know what I mean."

She sounded so sad that Andi reached out and squeezed her hand. "We're doing everything we can," she promised. "I'm the expert, remember? We'll find them, I'm sure of it."

She smiled encouragingly at Nina, who managed a watery smile in response.

After taking down a detailed description of the kittens, Ahyoka made a note of Nina's phone number.

"This really isn't the best place for kittens to get lost. I heard a pair of coyotes in my backyard last night, howling away. But if they stick together, they might be okay," she added, handing a stack of the freshly printed posters to Andi, who pinned one up on the bulletin board and put the rest in her bag. "I promise I'll call at once if I hear anything."

"We can't thank you enough for your help," Nina said.

Ahyoka looked a little sad. "I just hope that you find them soon," she said.

Her meaning was clear. *Before the coyotes do.*

Chapter Eight

Nina had obviously picked up on Ahyoka's concern, too. She was very quiet as they walked back to Santa Rosa Crafts.

"Maybe your mom has traced some of yesterday's customers," Andi said, trying to cheer them both up.

"Maybe," Nina said gloomily. "But most of our customers are tourists. Even if Mom finds some names, they might already have left town."

"We have to think positive," Andi urged. "It's one of the first rules of pet finding. We've had some cases back home that looked totally hopeless, but they turned out great in the end."

Nina looked a little happier. "As hopeless as this one?"

"Worse," Andi assured her. "We had to deal with a flash flood once when we were out looking for a missing pony! And when more than twenty animals disappeared from our local pet store, it took ages to find just *one*! Look, there's your mom. Let's see what she found out."

Angie Nelson had good news. "I have four names for you," she said triumphantly, waving a list at them.

Nina looked at the receipts. "The first three are for baskets that don't have lids, Mom," she said sadly. "The kittens could only have left the store in a basket with a lid, otherwise the customers would have noticed them."

"I didn't think of that." Angie took back the receipts and the list with a frown.

"One name is a start," Andi said, determined to stay positive. She looked at the receipt. "It looks like this customer bought several baskets. That should help our chances!" She read the name on Angie's list. "Helena Miller. Is this a local address?"

"Helena's one of our regular customers," Mrs. Nelson explained. "She's a beautician, and her salon is only two or three streets away from here. Listen, I have to head back to the riding center now, but call me if anything comes up, okay?"

Andi and Nina nodded, then dashed out the door. This was definitely a lead worth following up.

* * *

Helena Miller's beauty salon had a bright red-and-green awning, rows of hairdryers lined up along the back wall, a manicure bar by the window, and framed black-and-white photographs of movie stars on the walls.

"Those look like they came from your store," Andi said, pointing to a display of red-and-green baskets in the window.

The baskets had been filled with snowy white tissue paper, bottles of body lotion, and small packets of soap tied with red-and-green ribbons. The lids lay decoratively beside each basket.

Nina stood on tiptoe to peer into the display. "There's no sign of any kittens in those," she said.

"Maybe she bought some more baskets that she hasn't used yet," Andi suggested. She pushed open the door and led the way into the parlor's cool interior. "Hello? Ms. Miller?"

A tall woman with blond hair pinned neatly on top of her head looked up from the reception desk. "Can I help you?" she asked, smiling. "Oh, hello Nina! How are you?"

"Fine, thanks Ms. Miller," Nina said. "We're looking for some lost kittens, and wondered if we could ask you about the baskets you bought yesterday."

Nina explained how they thought the kittens may have been sold inside a basket by mistake. As Nina was talking, Andi took one of the posters out of her back-pack.

"How adorable!" the beautician exclaimed. "I'm sorry, but my baskets were empty. You can see them there in the window." She pointed to the display.

"Are you sure that when you took off the basket lids, the kittens weren't inside?" Andi checked. "They're very good at escaping when no one's looking."

Ms. Miller shook her head. "I would have noticed," she said. "And even if I hadn't, one of my customers certainly would have."

Andi rolled up the poster and began putting it back into her bag. But Helena Miller held out one of her elegantly manicured hands. "I'll put that in the store window if you like," she offered. "It's the least I can do."

"Thanks," Andi said gratefully, pushing the poster back across the desk.

"Do you have any more leads?" Ms. Miller asked.

"It's kind of hard to trace everyone who bought baskets yesterday," Nina admitted sadly. "Mom says there were lots of other customers, but they were tourists and paid in cash."

The beautician drummed her fingers on her desk. "Have you tried the local motels, or the campsite on the edge of town?" she suggested. "That's where most of the tourists stay."

"That's a really good idea!" Nina said. "My cousin Olivia works at the Sunny Inn. She might be able to help us."

"And if she can't, we can at least put up a few posters," Andi put in. She suddenly felt really grateful for all the help they were getting from the Tucson locals. Even though the city was bigger than Orchard Park, there was a real feeling of community spirit in Nina's neighborhood and enthusiasm about finding the missing pets. "Thanks, again, Ms. Miller. You've been a real help!"

It was a brisk fifteen-minute walk to the Sunny Inn. Nina and Andi walked down several residential streets, across a kids' playground, and past a row of convenience stores and a couple of warehouses. Soon, they could see the Sunny Inn's cheerful neon sign.

"Nina!" the girl on the reception desk greeted them. She had a cute heart-shaped face and sparkling green eyes behind funky tortoiseshell glasses. "Great to see you! To what do I owe the pleasure?"

"It's no pleasure, Olivia," Nina said glumly, after introducing Andi. She showed her cousin one of the posters. "We're looking for Mosi's kittens."

Olivia's face fell. "Those cute little things are missing?" she asked in dismay. "But they're so tiny and so helpless!"

To Andi's surprise, Nina's cousin looked close to tears. Nina glanced at Andi. "Olivia's kind of emotional," she whispered apologetically. "Listen Ol, it's not over yet. They're semi-feral, remember? They've got a better chance than many domesticated kittens would."

Nina's cousin sniffed and reached for a tissue. "Sorry," she gulped. "It's just — they're so cute and so small. . . . "

"Can we put up a poster?" Andi asked when Olivia started bawling.

Olivia wiped her eyes and reached for the poster. "You think they were sold in a *basket*?" she said in surprise, after reading the text. "Well, there's a woman at the motel who came in with a Santa Rosa Crafts bag yesterday afternoon."

"Is she still staying here?" Andi queried, suddenly feeling hopeful. "Could we speak with her?"

Olivia pinned the poster on the bulletin board behind the desk. "She's in room three-oh-five," she said, reaching for another tissue and blowing her nose. "Listen, I really hope you find them. Call me when you do, okay?"

Nina and Andi hurried across the parking lot to room

305, and Andi knocked tentatively on the door. It was opened by a young woman with cropped blond hair and a friendly smile. An untidy backpack stood by the door, packed close to bursting.

"I remember those kittens," she said, studying the poster. "They were curled up in a basket by the register."

"What time was that?" Andi asked.

"About three-thirty," the blond woman said promptly. "I noticed a store across the street with a large clock in the window just before I went in. You know, Santa Rosa Crafts is such a great little place!" she enthused. "I bought this cute bear." She showed Andi and Nina the carved stone bear, which held a miniature fish in its paws. "The white bear is a powerful healing object, perfect for my brother, who has problems with his back." She also showed them a tiny earthenware pot painted with an image of the moon. But it was so tiny that even Dezba's paw wouldn't have fit inside. "I have to buy small," she said, nodding at her bulging backpack. "I loved all the stuff at the store, but I don't have space for anything else."

"Another dead end," Nina sighed as they headed for the local campsite. "Is pet finding always like this?"

"We actually got some important information," Andi

pointed out. "Remember what that woman said about noticing the clock across the street? If we can figure out exactly *when* the kittens disappeared, we're more likely to find them."

"I guess," Nina said, sounding unconvinced. "Come on, we may as well check out the campsite. It's not far."

She led the way down a path edged with long yellow grass that was dotted with tiny flowers. Andi ran her hand along the furry tops of the grass, enjoying the tickling feeling on her fingers.

Nina stopped so suddenly that Andi almost bumped into her. "Listen," she hissed. "Can you hear something?"

Something was rustling in the grass beside the path. "That's bigger than a cicada," Andi said, hunkering down and peering into the growth. "Hey, there aren't any snakes around here, are there?"

Nina shrugged. "Some," she said. "But they don't rustle so loud."

Was it possible that the kittens had escaped from the campsite and were making their way home along the path? Andi shuffled forward, listening intently. Then —

"Whoa!" She scrambled to her feet as something resembling a very small pig came hurtling out of the grass toward them. "What's *that*?"

The hairy little creature cocked its ears and stared hard at Andi and Nina. The sunlight gleamed on its rough gray coat and a pair of very small, very sharp-looking tusks.

"It's a javelina," Nina said, grinning at the expression on Andi's face. "It means 'little spear' in Spanish."

"Because of its tusks, right?" Now that she'd gotten over her fright, Andi was fascinated. She wrinkled her nose. "It's pretty smelly. What is it, some kind of wild pig?"

Nina shook her head. "Actually, it's not related to the pig family at all," she said. "It has something to do with having a different number of toes and the way its tusks point down instead of up."

"Weird," Andi murmured. Now that she took a closer look at the javelina, she could see that it had a longer, finer snout than a pig. There was a collar of pale fur around its neck, and it had neat black legs and hooves.

The javelina had clearly decided the girls weren't a threat. It turned to the nearest prickly pear and took a bite out of a long fleshy leaf covered with ferocious spikes, chewing it like it was a marshmallow.

"I don't know about the kittens' chances if they bump into one of these guys," Andi remarked, looking at the javelina's sharp teeth and tusks.

"Don't worry, it's a vegetarian," Nina assured her. "They're pretty common around here. I guess they're cute in a way, but I wouldn't want one as a pet."

After one last suspicious glance at Andi and Nina, the javelina shuffled into the undergrowth and disappeared.

The campsite manager was a clean-shaven young man with his hair pulled back in a slick black ponytail. He hadn't seen the kittens, but he took three posters and promised to put them up around the site that afternoon. Glancing around the little white reception trailer with its view of the motor homes and brightly colored tents of the campsite, Andi suddenly thought of the British couple with their motor home who'd come into the store three days earlier. They had mentioned that they were staying at the local campsite. Andi knew they'd want to know about the kittens.

"The Tatfords?" the manager echoed when Andi asked about them. "British, right? We don't get too many British folks around here." He leaned his arms on the desk. "They headed for the Grand Canyon last night. I think they were planning on taking it easy and stopping off along the way. Tourists love that highway route. There's plenty to see. But we were sorry to see them go. They were real nice people."

"Yes, they were," Nina agreed. "Oh well. Could we ask around the campsite anyway, in case any of your guests were in my grandfather's store yesterday?"

"Sure, you can," said the man. "Good luck."

Nina knocked on the doors of the caravans and motor homes, while Andi checked out the tents. But there weren't many people around, and although the few tourists they met took an interest in the posters, they weren't able to help.

"Most people are probably out shopping," Nina guessed.

"Or hiking or doing some other kind of vacation stuff," Andi agreed.

They walked despondently toward the gates. A tourist in a large floral shirt and straw hat was coming out of the reception building ahead of them, carrying a shiny metal bucket.

"Excuse me, sir, but were you in Santa Rosa Crafts yesterday, by any chance?" Andi tried. "We're looking for three missing kittens."

The tourist took off his hat and scratched his thinning hair. "I've never heard of that store, but I did see a kitten today."

Andi's eyes widened. She looked at Nina.

"I walked down to the shopping district first thing,"

the tourist said slowly, backtracking through his day. "I got a coffee at that diner place, but it wasn't there, they had a dog. . . . "

Come on! Andi begged silently.

"It was the hardware store where I picked up this bucket!" he said at last. "The guy there had a kitten."

Chapter Nine

"Was it a brown tabby, like in the poster?" Andi checked.

The tourist studied the poster. "Yeah, kind of like that," he said.

"What was the name of the hardware store?" Nina prompted.

"Hudson, or Hobs, or something like that," the tourist said.

"Hobson?" Nina suggested.

"That's it!" the tourist agreed. "But, if you don't mind, I've gotta go fix my water tank. Good luck with your search!" He waved the bucket at them in farewell and strode into the campsite.

"Hobson's is only one street away from Santa Rosa Crafts!" Nina exclaimed. "You can reach it down the alley at the back of our store. The kittens could have easily escaped and made it to the hardware store on their own, or maybe Mr. Hobson found them in the alley! Come on, let's go check it out!"

"The guy said there was only one kitten," Andi warned, following Nina back down the path where they saw the javelina.

"He only *saw* one kitten," Nina corrected her. "The other two could have been hiding. Hardware stores are like our store — the kittens could find hundreds of hiding places!"

"That's true," Andi said. She didn't want to tell Nina the other two could be somewhere completely different. And if they had split up, the job of finding them was going to be three times harder.

"Come on!" Nina insisted, breaking into a run. Andi ran alongside her, glancing at the undergrowth in case the javelina put in another appearance. It had been pretty cute and unlike any wild creature she had seen before. But the long grass was silent.

They ran side by side all the way back into town. Andi enjoyed feeling the sun on her shoulders as she jogged along the dusty sidewalk. It reminded her of running back in Florida.

The first thing Andi noticed back at the store was that Tate wasn't in his usual sunny spot. She'd gotten used to seeing the old hunting dog lying below the store window with his eyes closed. The storefront seemed oddly empty without him.

"Where's Tate, Mr. Nelson?" she asked, as she and Nina headed for the kitchen and a long, cool drink of water.

Mr. Nelson was locking one of the jewelry cabinets. He took out the key and weighed it thoughtfully in one hand. His expression was unreadable. "That is an interesting question," he said. "And I'm afraid that I don't have an answer. He went for a walk this morning, but he hasn't come back yet."

"You mean Tate's missing, too?" Nina groaned. "No! Not now, with the kittens and everything!"

To Andi's dismay, Nina covered her eyes and burst into tears. Andi waited for Mr. Nelson to tell them that Tate wasn't missing, that he'd probably just gone wandering, but to her surprise he didn't. Instead, he put his arms around Nina and held her close. His eyes were dark and strangely serene, like he knew something that they didn't. Andi felt a lump in her throat, and she clenched her jaw to stop the tears from breaking through.

Nina sniffed. "Sorry." She gulped. "It's just — on top of losing the kittens, it seems so unfair."

Andi had a sudden, horrible thought. "What if Tate's been hit by a car or something?"

"Tate's a wise old dog," Mr. Nelson murmured. "He'll take care of himself."

"Don't you *care* about Tate?" Nina said, sounding angry. "He could be hurt! How can you just stand there and — "

Mr. Nelson held up his hand. "Enough."

"Enough?" Nina looked appalled. "Tate's *your dog*, Grandfather! How can you be so calm?"

Andi opened her mouth to make some suggestions about finding dogs. But there was a look in Mr. Nelson's eyes that stopped her. He did care about Tate — she knew he did. Maybe he just wasn't ready to talk about him yet. She'd seen other pet owners in denial when their pets first disappeared.

"Tell me, Nina," Mr. Nelson said firmly. "What have you and Andi been doing today?"

Andi knew they had to respect Mr. Nelson's feelings if he didn't want to talk about Tate.

"Someone saw a kitten in Hobson's today," Nina sniffed, wiping her eyes. "We thought we'd go and check it out." Her lip trembled again. "But what if it's not the right kitten? I don't think I can take any more bad news today."

"Good or bad, we have to find out," Andi told her. "It's another piece of the puzzle. You can't see the picture until the puzzle is finished, and every piece plays a part in the end."

Mr. Nelson gave Andi a wise nod, and Nina made a sad smile. "I guess you're right," she said.

Mr. Nelson got two glasses of ice water for the girls. He didn't say anything else about Tate. She guessed he must be feeling pretty anxious inside. She knew how fond he was of the old hunting dog. Or maybe he thought Tate would come wandering back in his own time.

When they were cooled off and a little calmer, Andi and Nina set off down the alley that led to Hobson's hardware store. The alley wound upward until Andi was treated to a view of all of Tucson, spreading as far as the distant dusty mountains surrounding the city. Although Nina's neighborhood had a cozy-village feel to it, the view reminded Andi of just how big the city of Tucson was in comparison to Orchard Park. She tried not to think about how much harder it was going to be to find the missing animals in a place this size.

Hobson's stood at the end of the alley, its storefront neatly painted dark blue. Brushes, plastic buckets, boxes of nails and bolts and screws, and a faded sign about fireworks were displayed in the window.

Nina glanced at Andi. "Think positive, right?" she said, biting her lip.

"Right," Andi said and gave her an encouraging high five.

They walked together into the dim, dusty interior. The store owner was sitting by the register with his boots on the desk and his nose deep in the sports section of the local newspaper.

"Hi, Mr. Hobson," said Nina.

The store owner swung his feet to the floor. "Hi, Nina," he said, giving Andi a friendly nod. "Not with your grandfather today?"

Nina shook her head. "I know this sounds kind of strange, Mr. Hobson," she began, "but can we see your kitten?"

Mr. Hobson looked puzzled. "My kitten? She only just got here. How do you know about her?"

"Someone told us they'd seen her," Nina said.

Andi gave her best smile. "We're crazy about animals," she gushed. "I hear your kitten is the cutest thing ever. Please can we see her? We won't stay long."

"Well, sure. If you want to!" Mr. Hobson said with a shrug. "Come on back."

He walked to the back of the store and pushed aside the curtain separating the store from his apartment.

"She's right there," he said, pointing to a large green chair by the window. A fluffy gray kitten sat up and looked at them with her head to one side.

"Oh, no!" Nina moaned. She sat heavily on the edge of the armchair and put her hands over her eyes. "It's the wrong kitten!"

"Is Nina okay?" Mr. Hobson asked Andi.

"She's just disappointed," Andi told him, feeling sick with disappointment, too. "She's lost three kittens, and we're trying to find them."

"That's too bad," Mr. Hobson said sympathetically. "Smokestack here came from a friend downtown. She was the last one in the litter. But, you know, I did hear of someone else who'd recently got some new kittens. Now who was it?"

Nina lifted her head.

"You did?" Andi said. "Where?"

Mr. Hobson thought hard. "Got it!" he exclaimed. "Dave — he works here Saturdays — told me that he served a couple who asked him where the pet store was, because they'd just gotten some kittens."

Andi looked at him. "Kitten*s*, with an 's'?" she checked, just to be sure.

Mr. Hobson nodded. "I'm pretty sure that's what Dave said."

"That could be really helpful!" Andi said, smiling at the store owner. She could tell he was still worried about Nina, who was staring out of the window. "Where's the pet store?"

"Oh, not far." The store owner pointed down the street. "Nina knows where it is, she'll show you."

After thanking Mr. Hobson several more times, Andi towed Nina outside. "This is a really good lead," she said, squeezing Nina's arm. "It's the first mention we've heard of more than one kitten!"

Nina shrugged. "If you say so."

Andi could tell that all the dead ends were beginning to get Nina down. "Pet finding is *always* like this," she explained. "If that tourist hadn't told us about the guy in the hardware store, we wouldn't have picked up this last clue. We'll find Mosi's kittens soon, I know it! And then we'll start looking for Tate."

Nina didn't look convinced. "The pet store's this way," she said gloomily. "Come on."

A delivery truck was parked outside the store with its back doors open. A young man in a blue T-shirt printed with the silhouette of a dog and the words PETS4EVER was unloading boxes of food, pet beds, and what looked like the frame of a new aquarium onto the sidewalk.

"He must work here," Andi figured, nudging Nina. "Excuse me?" She followed the man through the door, Nina close behind her.

"Not now, kid," he said, dumping an armful of boxes on the floor. "I'm busy."

"It won't take a minute," Andi insisted, following him back outside. "Do you remember someone coming into the store yesterday to buy stuff for some kittens?"

The man had disappeared back inside the truck. Andi and Nina waited patiently until he jumped back down with another box in his arms. It looked heavy.

"Maybe we should help him unload," Nina suggested.

Andi nodded. "Good plan. Hey do you want a hand?" she offered, taking one side of the box before the man could protest.

"I'll bring in some of these pet beds." Nina reached into the truck and piled up several of the beds until they wobbled alarmingly in her arms. "We really need to talk to you, sir."

"Okay," Blue T-shirt said. "Hey, Franco!" he called to the truck driver. "There's some stuff in the back I can't reach. Grab it for me, will ya?"

"Do you remember anyone coming in yesterday, asking about kittens?" Andi repeated, shifting the box so

that she had a better grip as they shuffled back inside the store.

"We can put it down here," the man said, nodding a clear space on the floor. "Kittens, you say? Yeah, there was someone who wanted to buy stuff for a new kitten."

Nina staggered into the store and almost tripped over the doormat, since she was completely unable to see her feet over the stack of pet beds. Andi reached her just in time to stop the beds from toppling to the floor and helped her set them down by the cash register.

"What were they like?" Andi prompted, turning back to the man, who was stacking cans of pet food onto a shelf.

"Who?" He reached into the box for some more cans.

"The people who came into the store and asked about kittens." Andi shot a frustrated glance at Nina.

He shrugged. "They came in, they bought blankets and droppers, they left. I didn't get much of a look at them."

"Did you get their names?" Nina asked hopefully.

The man straightened up. "What is this, twenty questions?" he grumbled. "We didn't introduce ourselves. They paid cash and left. Now, can I get back to work?"

Nina was about to ask another question, but Andi laid a hand on her shoulder. This wasn't getting them anywhere. "Well, thanks anyway," she said, struggling to keep the disappointment out of her voice. "Sorry we bothered you."

As they were heading out of the store, the man called them back. "I don't know if it's helpful," he said, "but they had some kind of accent. You know, like British or something?"

Andi whirled around. "British?" she echoed in astonishment. The Tatfords! Could they have anything to do with the kittens' disappearance?

"Let's call Mom and ask her if the Tatfords came into the store yesterday," Nina said, as they hurried back toward Santa Rosa Crafts.

Andi linked arms with her. "And maybe Tate will have come home by now," she suggested.

But, back at the store, there was still no sign of the old dog. Mr. Nelson was calmly arranging a stack of rugs as they came through the door.

"Hi, you two," he said. "What do you think of this display? Too much red? Should I mix it up a little more?"

Andi was puzzled. She knew Mr. Nelson loved his dog. Why was he acting like nothing had happened? He hadn't even asked if they'd seen him.

If Nina was troubled by the way her grandfather was

behaving, she gave no sign. "We have a new lead on the kittens, Grandfather!" she said. "Can I call Mom and ask her something?"

"Of course," said Mr. Nelson. "Perhaps you could give me a hand arranging the window, Andi."

She wanted to ask Mr. Nelson how he was feeling about Tate, but she suddenly felt shy and couldn't figure out the right way to ask. Instead, she busied herself lifting the rugs and draping them over one another until they made a beautiful fan of color.

Nina hung up the phone. "The Tatfords did come in!" she said. "Mom says she definitely remembers their British accents. They browsed a while, but the phone rang out back, and when Mom came back from answering it, they had gone."

"What time was that?" Andi asked.

"About four o'clock," Nina replied.

Everything was fitting into place! The kittens had still been in the store at three-thirty — the blond woman at the Sunny Inn had been positive about the time. But one major thing was worrying Andi. The Tatfords had seemed so nice! Could they really be kitten thieves?

"You can never tell what people are really like when you only meet them once," Nina said, guessing what

Andi was thinking. "Come on, we'd better get over to the campsite. We have to talk to them!"

Andi gasped. "But we can't! The campsite guy said they left last night for the Grand Canyon!" She stared at Nina in dismay. "What are we going to do now?"

Chapter Ten

"I seem to have a knack for appearing at the wrong time." Mr. Talbot was standing in the doorway, holding his car keys. "What's wrong? You two look like you've been hit by a truck."

"Everything's wrong!" Andi burst out. "We just keep reaching dead ends, Dad. We think we know who took the kittens, but if we're right, they've already left town for the Grand Canyon and taken the kittens with them in their camper."

Mr. Talbot looked astonished. "You found out who took the kittens?"

"We're as sure as we can be," Andi said. "I mean, we don't have any proof, but we've checked everything else and it just fits."

"You can't accuse people without proof," Mr. Talbot warned. "Do you have a motive?"

"No," Andi said helplessly. "Unless you count how cute the kittens are. We've been following the trail all day. We checked out a lead that took us out of town to the motel, then the campsite, then back again to the hardware store a block away, then to the pet store, and now back here. We were *this close*, Dad," she said, pinching her fingers together for emphasis.

Mr. Talbot looked dumbfounded. "You followed that whole chain of clues? And you ended up with an answer! It sounds like this theory is worth pursuing, then."

Andi shrugged. "Not if the kittens have gone all the way to the Grand Canyon. They might as well be on the moon."

Mr. Talbot came over and rested his hands on Andi's shoulders. "I'm very proud of you, Andi," he said. "Coming this far has taken a lot of persistence and brainpower. I can't believe you didn't give up." He paused, and gave a wry smile. "Well actually, I can. You're as determined as your mom when you put your mind to it, aren't you?"

Andi forced a smile. "I guess." She turned to Nina. "Sorry it turned out like this. I really thought we'd find them, you know?"

"Who's giving up?" Mr. Talbot demanded. "You need someone to drive you to the Grand Canyon? I'll do it!"

Andi stared at him. "But it's three hundred miles away!" she protested. "Don't you have a meeting this afternoon?"

"I'll call and postpone it," Mr. Talbot said, digging in his pocket for his cell phone.

"You'd do that for me?" Andi said in disbelief. "So I can find some kittens?"

Mr. Talbot looked up from punching in the number. "That's what dads are for," he said simply. "Your dedication has really impressed me, Andi. You've shown logic, and common sense, and most of all, persistence. That's worth at least three hundred miles in my book." He put the phone down for a moment and got a little more serious. "But we can't possibly scout the whole canyon, you know. It's too big. We'll scour the road for campers on the way up and then check the southern campgrounds."

Andi got a lump in her throat so big that it threatened to choke her. "Dad—" she began, but Nina interrupted.

"The guy with the ponytail at the campsite reception said the Tatfords were going to take it easy along the way. We might not have to go as far as the Grand Canyon, after all. I'll make sandwiches and fill some water bottles. Oh, and we need a map! We're really going after them? I can't believe it! Mr. Talbot, you're the best!"

Andi smiled. *Just what I was going to say*, she thought.

"Are you going to stay overnight somewhere?" Mr. Nelson asked, stepping down from the window as Nina dashed back to the kitchen.

Mr. Talbot shook his head. "I can only take the rest of today off. Hopefully we'll catch up to them since they're in a camper and driving slower. But if for any reason we need to drive through to the canyon itself, we'll get back pretty late."

"We'd better get moving!" Andi exclaimed, checking her watch. "It's past eleven already."

"The Tatfords will probably be taking it slow, like Nina said," Mr. Nelson said. "You should check all the campsites along the way, in case you end up passing them. And there's a new campsite a couple of hours out of town — it won't be on your map because it only opened last month. It's by a waterfall. Make sure you look there."

Andi nodded and made a note on the back of an old store receipt.

Nina brought out a cooler full of food and bottled drinks. She also pulled the cardboard box and blanket out from under the kitchen table, in case they really did find the kittens and needed a safe way to bring them home. Then, after Andi's dad had finished his phone call and they'd said goodbye to Mr. Nelson, Nina and Andi followed him out to the Jeep.

"They would have taken this road first, up to Flagstaff." Nina pointed to the map.

"Here we go, then," Mr. Talbot declared and swung out onto the road.

Soon the dusty sprawl of Tucson was behind them and the Jeep was powering north along the desert highway. Mr. Talbot put on the radio, but unlike the trip to the Canyon de Chelly, Nina and Andi were too busy planning to sing along.

"It looks like there are campsites here and here," Andi said, pointing to the symbols on the map.

"And we can't forget that new place Grandfather mentioned, with the waterfall," said Nina. "I hope there's a sign on the highway for it."

Andi stared out of the window. Cacti decorated the landscape, their spiny arms stretched out just like in the movies, and she remembered that she still had to buy a cactus for her room. The time she and her dad had spent painting the furniture felt like a lifetime ago.

"Look, there's a diner coming up!" Nina shaded her eyes against the sun. "Maybe the Tatfords stopped off for something to eat."

"Maybe, but if they stopped here, they're long gone

by now," said Mr. Talbot. "There are no motor homes in the parking lot."

Sure enough, the parking lot contained only two or three battered pickups and another Jeep. They drove straight past and on through the desert.

They soon passed a small convenience store and a gas station. Andi didn't see a single person at either place. It was as if they had all been blown away by the wind.

They ate their sandwiches on the move and crunched through some juicy green apples. At last, they saw a new-looking sign to a campsite.

"This must be the one with the waterfall," Nina said, studying the map as Mr. Talbot turned off the highway and they bumped along down a pitted cement road. "The river's marked here, see?"

After jolting along the road for a couple of miles, they found themselves on a grassy river bank. There were a few trees by the water's edge, and shade was provided by a craggy cliff. A spectacular waterfall cascaded down the cliff face into a dark blue pool. Several motor homes and tents were grouped around the pool, and one or two people were swimming.

"It's beautiful!" Andi exclaimed. She thought longingly about diving in as they climbed out of the Jeep.

"Not too long, girls," Mr. Talbot warned. "We're not sightseeing. Twenty minutes max."

Andi forced her mind back to the missing kittens. She and Nina ran into the campsite. At first glance, the motor homes all looked the same. Were they going to have to knock on every single door? If the Tatfords weren't here, they didn't have the time to hang around. They needed some kind of clue — anything. . . .

"Andi!" Nina squealed, pointing. "Look at that flag!"

The distinctive red, white, and blue design of the British Union Jack hung in the window of a large motor home parked in the shade of the cliff. Andi and Nina raced toward it — and stopped dead when they saw a little girl, about five years old, sitting on the steps.

"Er, hi," Andi said uncertaïnly. "Is your last name Tatford?"

The little girl stared at them. "Mummy!" she called. "Someone's here to talk to you!"

Mummy? Andi frowned. Jane Tatford looked too old to have a girl this young.

"What's the matter, darling?" A dark-haired woman in a bright orange blouse poked her head out of the motor home. She had a pleasant-sounding British accent. "Oh, hello. Can I help you?"

It wasn't Jane Tatford. Although Andi wasn't really

surprised, she couldn't stop her heart from sinking into her sneakers.

"I'm sorry for disturbing you," she said. "We're looking for a British couple with the last name Tatford. Do you know if there are any other British people at this campsite?"

The woman shook her head. "We've only just arrived," she said. "And I'm pretty sure we're the only British people here. Sorry."

Just in case she was wrong, Andi and Nina searched the rest of the campsite for a motor home with some kind of British clue — or three adorable kittens. But it was clear that the Tatfords weren't there.

"That's too bad," Mr. Talbot said as Andi and Nina climbed back into the Jeep. "Hang in there, guys. Maybe we'll have better luck at the next site."

Andi reached over and squeezed his shoulder. Even though she was desperately worried about the kittens, it felt great to be pet finding with her dad!

Back on the highway, the road shimmered in the afternoon heat. They drove in silence through the rock-strewn landscape. There wasn't another car in sight. The scenery was dramatic and desolate now, with craggy mountains rising on either side.

Up ahead, Andi caught the flash of a reflector band. Three workmen in hard hats were sitting in the back of their truck, which was parked at an angle across the highway.

Mr. Talbot slowed the Jeep as one of the men hopped off the back of the truck and waved.

"Sorry," the workman said. "You can't get through this way."

"What do you mean, we can't get through?" Andi gasped. "We have to get to the Grand Canyon!"

The workman tipped back his hat. "Maybe you do, but you'll have to go the long way around," he said. "There's been a rock fall. We're working on it, but this section of the highway is closed until tomorrow morning. You'll have to take this road instead, and rejoin the highway farther up." He pointed to a small road leading off to the left.

"But this goes up into the mountains," Nina said, dismayed. "It could take hours to get back to the highway, and the Tatfords could be way ahead of us by then."

"It doesn't look like we have a choice," Mr. Talbot pointed out. "Let's hope that the Tatfords had to come this way, too."

They followed the new road as it twisted up through

crags and bluffs, the Jeep's engine grinding in a low gear for much of the climb. When they reached the top of the incline, the view across the desert made them all gasp. Andi stared at the road on the far side of the rock fall, snaking like a thin gray thread, but she couldn't see anything that looked like a motor home. Maybe the campsite manager had been wrong. Maybe the Tatfords were in a hurry to get to the Grand Canyon after all.

The road got increasingly narrow and rocky, and soon they found themselves driving so close to the edge of a cliff that Andi had to close her eyes.

"This can't be right," Mr. Talbot muttered, bringing the Jeep to a halt and reaching for the map. "We seem to be heading farther and farther away from the highway. We should have seen another sign by now."

"It's four o'clock already," Nina said desperately. "At this rate we'll have to turn around and go back to Tucson before we reach the canyon. What are we going to do?"

Straight ahead of them, the road forked in two. There was a sign on the right-hand fork.

SCULPTURE GALLERY

NATIVE CRAFTS

HAND-THROWN SALT-GLAZE POTS FOR SALE

Andi stared at the sign for a few moments. There was something about the words that was made her fingers tingle. Was it the line about sculpture? Or salt-glaze pots! Yes, that was it!

"Dad, we've got to take the right-hand fork," she said. "Mr. Tatford commented specifically on pottery at Santa Rosa Crafts, remember?"

"Yes! He talked about a salt glaze!" Nina recalled, looking at Andi with a flash of hope in her eyes.

Mr. Talbot checked his watch. "We've already lost an hour on this diversion," he warned. "It doesn't say how far this gallery is. Are you sure you want to risk it?"

"It's just a hunch," Andi admitted, "but we've come this far. I say we go for it."

Mr. Talbot nodded. "Whatever you say, boss," he murmured as he turned the Jeep to follow the sign for the gallery.

They bumped down the rutted road. After about ten minutes, Andi spotted a neat wooden building nestled into the mountainside, surrounded by forests. Large sculptures in rock and bronze and strange, twisted pieces of wood stood beneath the trees. Andi crossed her fingers and grabbed Nina's hand.

Mr. Talbot slowed the Jeep and turned around a corner into a small parking lot. A sparkling white motor home was tucked up against the gallery building, and fluttering on a clothes line beside it were two Disney-World T-shirts and three pairs of white socks.

"Tacky T-shirts," Nina murmured, shading her eyes. "They have to belong to tourists."

"That motor home has Florida plates!" Andi said, recognizing the teal and orange Miami colors. A rush of hope flooded through her. "The Tatfords said they started their trip in Miami!"

The motor home's rear window sat just above the license plate, and there in the sunlight were three tiny fluffy shapes bundled against the glass, their little pink mouths opening and closing in silent meows.

"It's them!" Andi yelled, scrambling out of the Jeep.

"I can see Nascha!" Nina said, racing after Andi toward the motor home. "Look, in the window! And there's Dezba — and Yas, too! Andi, we've found them! We've found them!"

Chapter Eleven

The kittens stood up curiously, put their paws against the glass, and stared at them.

"It's really them!" Nina said, half crying and half laughing. "I can't believe we found them!"

Andi felt slightly dazed as she peered into the dim interior of the Tatfords' motor home. A few minutes ago, they'd been lost in the mountains with no sign of the couple or the missing kittens anywhere. Then she'd followed a hunch about Mr. Tatford's love of pottery, and now they were standing in a hidden mountain valley, hundreds of miles from Tucson, staring at precisely what they'd come to find!

"How are we going to get them out of there?" she asked.

Nina tried the door of the motor home. It was unlocked. "Simple," she declared. "The Tatfords stole them from us, so we're going to go in there and steal them back!"

"You can't." Andi warned, putting a hand on Nina's shoulder as she began to climb up the steps. "You're not thinking straight, Nina. You can't just walk into someone's motor home like you own it! We'd better wait for the Tatfords to come back, and then we can ask them what they're doing with the kittens."

"You're absolutely right, Andi," Mr. Talbot said, walking over to join them. "There's probably a perfectly rational explanation, and we owe it to the Tatfords to hear them out."

Reluctantly, Nina let go of the door handle. They all looked at the kittens in the window again. Nascha was still leaning up against the glass, her mouth open in a plaintive meow. Dezba and Yas had gone to sleep, curled up together in a tangle of tabby and white fur.

"Jim, look who it is!" a voice suddenly exclaimed behind her. "It's the girls from that lovely craft shop!"

Andi spun around. Jim and Jane Tatford were walking across the grass toward them. Andi searched their faces for signs of guilt or embarrassment, but they just looked surprised.

"This is a most extraordinary coincidence!" Jim Tatford declared. "Have you come to look at the pots?"

Andi was floored. They were supposed to look guilty, not happy to see them! "Er, we came to get the kittens back," she said awkwardly.

Jane Tatford looked confused. "You want them *back*?" she said. "But I thought you wanted to get rid of them."

It was Nina's turn to look surprised. "We never said that," she protested.

Everyone started talking at once. Mr. Tatford waved his arms for silence. "I think you'd better come inside for a cup of tea," he said. "It looks like we've all got our wires crossed."

Inside, the motor home was cozy and comfortable, with plush carpeting and soft tartan seats. Dezba and Nascha immediately jumped down from the window and padded over to say hello, while Yas stayed snoozing on the sill. Nina and Andi kneeled on the seat to play with them, laughing as Dezba pounced on their fingers. Mrs. Tatford switched on the kettle and Mr. Tatford found some cookies in one of the tiny cupboards.

"I don't know what to say." Mr. Tatford looked rather flustered as he passed around a plate of cookies. "We thought we'd be doing you a favor by taking the kittens off your hands. Your grandfather talked about you getting rid of them!"

"You mean when he was upset while you were looking

around? He only meant we should take them out back. Mr. Nelson doesn't like the kittens getting in the way of customers," Andi explained.

"But we thought that with the mother cat out of the picture, it was only a matter of time before the kittens would be in danger from snakes and coyotes," Mrs. Tatford put in anxiously. "When we went back to the store, the lady in there was so rushed off her feet that we felt we had to do something to help. Didn't you see our note?"

Nina looked at them in surprise. "You left a note?" she asked.

"Yes, right on that big stack of rugs by the door." Mrs. Tatford frowned. "Gosh, how dreadful for you if you never got it."

"It must have blown out of the door!" Andi guessed. "Your mom said it was a windy day, Nina."

"Oh, I'm so sorry." Mrs. Tatford looked horrified. "What must you have thought of us?"

"We didn't know what to think," Andi said, deciding it would be tactful not to admit the conclusion they'd jumped to.

Mr. Tatford was still looking confused. "But, Nina, you said something about not being able to keep them forever, didn't you? So what's going to happen to them?"

"I love them dearly, but it's not up to me if they stay at the store," Nina said. "I have to respect their wild nature. Their mother will come back one day, and then the kittens will decide if they want to follow her back to the desert. It's their choice, however much I want them to stay with me forever. But I would never leave them in danger! I'm going to keep them inside until they're older, and then I'll let them run in the yard at night, just so they get used to the idea." She swallowed. "I have to give them the chance to leave, even though it breaks my heart."

Mrs. Tatford reached over and patted her hand. "Sweetheart, I'm really sorry for making you unhappy. I never dreamed the kittens meant this much to you!"

"What were you going to do with them at the end of your vacation?" Andi asked the Tatfords.

"Take them home with us, hopefully," Mr. Tatford said. "We have friends who brought a cat over from the States, and she dealt with the quarantine regulations very well. We thought we could do the same with these three."

There were certainly plenty of signs that the Tatfords knew how to take care of cats. Andi spotted a clean litter tray in one corner, and there was a comfortable fleece-lined basket under the table.

"We're big supporters of global animal charities," Mrs. Tatford went on, picking up Yas and stroking his golden tummy. "Giving these kittens a home seemed like the right thing to do at the time."

"I'm so sorry about the misunderstanding," Nina apologized, "but we'd really like to take them home. The kittens are wanted, I promise. I'm so sorry I didn't make that clear."

Mrs. Tatford blinked, as if she was trying not to cry. "Of course you must take them," she said. "I can see now that we completely misread the situation. We'll miss them terribly, but I know you have their best interest at heart." She pulled a handkerchief from her sleeve and blew her nose.

"And they have been quite restless cooped up in here," Mr. Tatford confessed, scooping Nascha up off the floor and handing her to Andi. "They'll be happier back in the store, with room to play."

"However did you find us?" Mrs. Tatford asked. "We camped in the desert last night, and you can't see this gallery from that little mountain road. I still can't believe you're here!"

"Andi's great at following clues," Nina told her. "We tracked down the pet store where you bought supplies for the kittens, then followed you on the road to the Grand Canyon because we knew that was where you were going next. When we got diverted off the main road, we saw that sign and remembered Mr. Tatford talking about a salt glaze on one of our pots."

"Goodness!" Mr. Tatford looked astounded. "Fancy remembering something like that! You two should be private detectives."

Andi smiled. "Well, I belong to the Pet Finders Club back home in Seattle," she said. "We do this kind of thing all the time — finding pets, I mean. Not following people across the desert!"

Mr. Talbot grinned at her. "Just as well. I can't see your mom would be too happy if you made this a regular event!" He glanced at his watch. "We need to get going. Do you think these little ones are ready to leave?" He nodded toward the kittens.

"I guess so!" said Nina, cuddling Nascha close to her chin.

Mr. Talbot ducked out to get the cardboard box from the Jeep. The Tatfords helped to settle the kittens on the blanket inside before Andi carefully carried the box out of the motor home.

"You must take this," said Mrs. Tatford, handing Nina

the fleece-lined pet bed and a shopping bag containing a packet of kitten food and two empty bowls. "It'll only take up room in the van."

"Oh, thank you! They'll love this bed," Nina said. "We're really, really sorry about the mix-up. You've been so understanding, and I can see that the kittens mean a lot to you."

"Such is life," Mr. Tatford said bravely. "We shouldn't have taken them. I'm so sorry you never saw the note, and I'm sorry you had to come all this way to retrieve them. Perhaps we could stay in touch by e-mail? We'd love to hear how the kittens are getting on."

"I'll send you photos," Nina promised, writing down the Tatfords' e-mail address on a scrap of paper Mr. Tatford handed her.

"You will take good care of them, won't you?" Mrs. Tatford said, with a catch in her voice as she watched Andi load the box of kittens into the Jeep.

"Don't worry," Andi said with a smile, climbing in beside the kittens and leaning out of the window to say good-bye. Next to her, Dezba butted the flaps on the box with her head, looking for a way out. "If Dezba ever meets a coyote, I think it's the coyote who'll be in trouble!"

* * *

The journey back to Tucson seemed much shorter than the drive out, but it was still almost sunset by the time they reached Santa Rosa Crafts. Mr. Talbot parked the Jeep outside and helped Andi and Nina carry the box of wriggling kittens into the store. Nina undid the flaps and the kittens tumbled out one after the other, sniffing excitedly at all the familiar smells.

"I can't believe you found them!" Angie exclaimed, hugging Nina and Andi both at once. "We'd never have gotten them back if it hadn't been for you, Andi."

Mr. Talbot put his arm around Andi and pulled her close. "I'm really proud of you," he said softly. "The way you kept looking for the kittens, even though you must have felt like giving up a lot of the time — that's really something, Andi. Everyone is lucky you've started your Pet Finders Club."

Andi hugged him back. "It was a pretty wild desert dash, huh?" she joked. "And I guess you're an official pet finder now, Dad. Welcome to the club."

Dakota Nelson walked across the store toward them. Nina flew into his arms, and he kissed her on the top of her head. "I see that you found those rascals," he commented. "They look bigger, and I'm sure they will be twice as much trouble."

"You don't fool me, Grandfather," Nina scolded.

"You're as happy to see them as I am. And they'll quiet down as they get older, I promise."

"Is there any news on Tate?" Andi asked hopefully. "Now we've found the kittens, we can really concentrate on looking for him," she added. "We'll make some more posters. And do door-to-door questioning! Everyone knows him in the neighborhood. There are bound to be some really great leads."

Mr. Nelson rested his dark eyes on her. "Come with me, both of you," he said, holding out his hands. "I have something to show you."

Nina gazed at her grandfather. "You have bad news, don't you?" she said in a trembling voice. "I can tell from your face."

Mr. Nelson led Andi and Nina into the backyard. The crimson sun was hanging low in the sky, spreading warm coppery light through the clouds. "You need no gold when you have the sunset. It is riches in itself. I am happy to know that the sky is full of my ancestors. And I am happy that Tate is with them now.

Andi felt her heart miss a beat.

"Mr. Hobson called me," Mr. Nelson went on. "He found Tate underneath a bush in his yard."

"Dead?" Nina whispered.

Dakota nodded. "He was an old dog, Nina. He had a good long life, and he didn't suffer any pain."

"But he died on his own!" Nina protested, tears welling in her eyes. "That wouldn't have happened if we'd found him in time. No one should die alone."

"Dogs share many things with their ancestors, the wolves," Mr. Nelson said. "Wolves choose to leave the pack when it is their time to die. It is nature's way."

Andi's heart felt like it was breaking. She didn't trust herself to speak, so she just reached out and held Nina's hand.

"Tate knew that his life was at its end," Mr. Nelson said gently. "Think how he has been slowing down recently. I could see in his eyes that he was ready to leave us, and I was just waiting him to go for a walk one day and not come back. There was nothing I could have done to stop him — and it would not have been fair to try. He wanted to die outside, in the world that he loved so much."

Tears rushed into Andi's eyes, blurring her vision. "I'm sorry, Mr. Nelson," she choked out. "So sorry."

"It is the natural way of things," Mr. Nelson said. He pointed at the flaming sun. "Tate's spirit is in the sky now, hunting cloud rabbits and running with the wind.

There is a Navajo song that explains it better than I can. I will translate it for you." And he began to sing.

When it comes your time to die,
Be not like those whose hearts
Are filled with fear of death,
So that when their time comes
They weep and pray for a little more time
To live their lives over again
In a different way.
Sing your death song and
Die like a hero going home.

Mr. Nelson let the last note hang in the air. As if the sun had heard his song, it disappeared abruptly behind the mountains and darkness began to settle over the desert.

Andi's eyes swam with tears. Tate was the first pet she hadn't found. Everything Mr. Nelson had said, everything in the beautiful song, rang true, but it was a bitter truth all the same.

Andi spent the last day of her vacation with her dad, putting the finishing touches on her room. She had found the perfect cactus at the local garden center, and it looked great in the corner of her room. Then she and her dad had gone shopping for little New Year's gifts for Andi's mom and friends back in Orchard Park. Andi had found two fantastic masks — a rattlesnake and a fairy — that she planned to give to Tristan and Natalie to wear at Tristan's New Year's Eve party. She'd found one for herself, too — a tabby cat mask, to remind her of Mosi's kittens. She got a scented candle for her mom and bought her dad a set of paints. "So you can take those art lessons you mentioned," she explained as she gave them to him.

Mr. Talbot was delighted. "No more excuses!" he agreed, examining the neat rows of colored tubes in the box. Andi could see that he was already planning a painting in his mind. She hoped it wasn't going to be entirely blue.

Now, at last, it was time to head for the airport. Andi stared around the little room, trying to imprint the colorful blankets, the yellow cushions and blue furniture, the green baskets and incense burner on the windowsill in her mind. She'd never found a rug — perhaps because in her heart, she knew the tree of life rug would have been perfect.

"You must remember to water the cactus," she told her dad, shouldering her bag.

"Cacti don't need water," her dad pointed out with a grin. "That's why they live in deserts, remember?"

"Okay, but you have to dust it. Promise?" Andi begged. She hugged her dad tightly. "I've had such a great time," she said, resting her head on his shoulder. "Thanks for everything, Dad. You're the best!" She really meant it. She couldn't wait to see her mom and Buddy again, but it was sad having to leave her dad and this magical place behind.

Her dad hugged her back. "Come and see me again soon," he said. "Maybe next time we'll get to the Grand Canyon for real — without having to chase any missing kittens on the way." His eyes were twinkling, but Andi didn't mind him teasing her any more. He understood what pet finding meant to her now.

They passed Santa Rosa Crafts on the way to the airport, and Andi asked her dad to let her drop in and say goodbye to the Nelsons one more time. The kittens raced up to the door and tumbled around her feet, watched indulgently by Mr. Nelson, who was standing by the cash register.

"Careful, little one!" Andi laughed at Dezba, who was trying to nip her ankles. "Are you a kitten or a tiger cub?" She stroked Nascha's pale, pretty head and tickled Yas on his golden tummy one last time. This had been one of the most amazing pet hunts ever. Andi cast her mind over the long, twisting trail of clues, mountain roads, and misunderstandings that had finally led them to the kittens more than three hundred miles from where they started. It was incredible that they'd found them at all!

And Tate — Andi swallowed as she thought of the gentle, old hunting dog. As Mr. Nelson said, it had been his time to die, like a hero going home. It was important to remember Tate's long happy life, not his death.

"I'm glad you stopped by. I have a gift that I can give you in person now," Nina said shyly, coming through the beaded curtain with something held behind her back. "To say thank you for everything, and so you don't forget about us."

To Andi's delight, Nina was holding a silver squash blossom necklace. The Navajo girl reached out and put it around Andi's neck, where it felt warm and heavy.

"Thank you!" Andi exclaimed. "It's beautiful. But really, you don't need to thank me. And there's no way I'll ever forget you!"

"And I, too, have something to give you," said Mr. Nelson. "You loved this, and so now it is yours."

Andi stared in astonishment as Nina's grandfather reached behind the counter and lifted out the beautiful tree of life rug. "I don't know what to say," she stammered. "Thank you doesn't seem like enough."

Mr. Nelson smiled. "It is plenty," he said, as he helped Mr. Talbot roll it up for the Jeep ride. "Go safely, and visit us again soon."

"I will," Andi promised.

There was a hoarse, unkittenlike meow at the back of the store then. They all turned. Andi saw a thin sand-colored cat standing warily in the kitchen, looking through the beaded curtain at them. It was the cat she'd seen on her very first evening in Tucson.

"Mosi!" Nina said in surprise. "Boy, are we glad to see you! Your kittens have been such troublemakers. . . . "